HOOPED

A NOVEL BY
– MICHAEL BAINS –

This is a work of fiction. Names, characters, places, and incidents either are the product of the author's imagination or are used fictitiously.

Copyright © 2020 by Michael Bains

All rights reserved. No part of this book may be reproduced or used in any manner without written permission of the copyright owner except for the use of quotations in a book review. For more information, contact: hooped@michaelbains.ca.

First paperback edition November 2020

ISBN: 978-1-7772133-0-5 (paperback)
ISBN: 978-1-7772133-1-2 (ebook)

www.michaelbains.ca

Dedication

This book is dedicated to Tupac Shakur and Ermias "Nipsey Hussle" Asghedom. I'm attracted to the real, and these two were as real as they come.

- 1 -

JIMMY SAT ON the couch in a haze of alcohol and weed. He felt good. More numb than anything. But good nonetheless.

"Jimmy!" He looked up and saw Gary yelling in his direction. "Time for another shot."

Jimmy grinned but only relaxed deeper into the couch. "I'm good, brah. I'm way too high right now."

Gary walked over and held his hand out. "Come on, Captain," Gary said. "Don't let us down."

He grabbed Gary's hand and was pulled up and off his feet. Jimmy shook his head a few times to lessen the fog. It was the weed more than the booze that had him in a different zone.

Jimmy approached the bar, where shots were already lined up. Mounted overtop of the bar was a cabinet that ran the full length of the wall. It contained the finest scotch, whiskey, and gin available. Jimmy could picture his dad salivating at all the single malts.

Mike was pouring shots of cheap vodka from a sixty-ouncer of Absolut. His dad wouldn't let them touch any of his more expensive bottles, and they weren't stupid enough to try. "You guys wouldn't be able to appreciate the good stuff," Mike's dad had said. "Stick to this," thrusting the Absolut at them.

He was right. None of them really cared what they were drinking as long as it was free and would get them drunk.

Jimmy's friends were pouring a separate glass of 7-Up or Coke to chase down the alcohol, but Jimmy didn't need that.

He enjoyed the burning sensation trickling down his throat and into his chest. It was how he knew he was about to get messed up.

"Boys and girls," Mike slurred. "This might be the final Christmas dinner we get to have. We're all graduating next year, but I just want to let you know…" Mike was swaying back and forth at this point.

Karen put her hand on his back, then reached for his shot. "I think you've had enough."

Mike took a quick step away from her. "Cheers bitches!" and then he slammed back his shot.

Karen just shook her head.

"Cheers!" everyone else yelled.

They were in Mike's dad's basement. He was usually very protective of his man cave and didn't allow people down there without him present. There was only one exception: their annual basketball Christmas dinner.

It had been a tradition at Mike's since grade eight. The night would commence on the main floor, with all the boys and girls from each of the basketball teams and their girlfriends and boyfriends. Mike's mom would cook so much food that she'd pack each of the boys a container to take home. In grade ten, Jimmy and Gary had convinced Mike's dad to allow them a little taste of his liquor cabinet. By grade eleven, almost everybody at the Christmas dinner had a taste. And this year, everybody was drinking like seasoned drunks.

Jimmy heard his phone vibrate in his pocket and pulled it out. "Hello?"

"Whatup, G," Sunny replied. "How's the kiddie party?"

"Haha, it's pretty bumpin'. Drinks are flowing."

"Shit, eh. Should we crash it? Me and Ajay are just cruising."

Jimmy felt himself hesitate, and he knew Sunny could sense it too. "Uhh."

Sunny chuckled. "What? You embarrassed of us, bro?"

"Nah, nah, it's not that. Just no one here knows you. I'll come meet up with you guys."

"Yeah? Alright, we'll be there in ten. Be outside."

Sunny hung up before Jimmy had a chance to respond. He placed his phone back in his pocket and looked around the room. Jimmy was tall and lean with an athletic build. He would usually spike up his naturally messy hair and did his best to maintain a beard. He had a strong jaw and could pass off for being a few years older than he actually was. He'd never had problems attracting girls, but these days, he only had eyes for one.

He found Jessica talking to Paul, who seemed to be rambling on about something. Jimmy could feel his heart begin to race. Paul was Jessica's ex-boyfriend. They had dated briefly before Jimmy and Jessica, and now Jimmy had to see him every day at basketball practice.

Jessica noticed Jimmy looking over, and then Paul realized Jimmy's eyes were locked on him. Jessica smiled gently at Paul and then made her way over to Jimmy. Paul slunk away.

"Hi," she said, batting her eyelashes and gazing up at him.

"Hi. Talking to Mr. Perfect, I see?"

"Come on, Jimmy. You know me and Paul are still friends. We do have to see each other almost every day at school council."

"I know, I know. I'm just messing around." Jimmy stepped closer and put his hands on either side of her hips. "So how's your night?"

"Couldn't be more perfect," she smiled.

He slowly leaned in while pulling Jessica close. When their bodies met, Jessica stood on tiptoe while Jimmy bent forward. Their lips met in the middle. Jimmy indulged in the softness of the kiss and enjoyed the sweet taste of her lips. He wasn't a fan of PDA, but alcohol always made exceptions.

When they separated, she continued to look into his eyes and now wore a curious expression. "So how many joints you smoke tonight?"

Jimmy realized that his eyes were probably bloodshot. "One... or two. You upset?"

"Only that you didn't ask me."

Jimmy grinned. He knew she wasn't mad. It took a lot to upset Jess, and him smoking weed was hardly a trigger. "Did you actually want to? It was just me and Gary."

Jessica shrugged. She didn't particularly enjoy it but still did it from time to time, mainly because she knew how much Jimmy loved it.

Jimmy heard his phone vibrating in his pocket again and knew Jessica could hear it too. Jimmy silenced it and returned his gaze to Jessica. "I gotta take off tonight."

"Sunny?" He could hear the disappointment in her voice.

Jimmy nodded. "He's just dropping me at home. I don't think anyone else here is going to be able to drive."

"I can get my mom to drop you off. She's picking me up soon."

"Don't worry about it. He's already here. Thanks, though." He leaned in and gave Jess a peck on the lips. "Talk to you tomorrow?"

Jessica just nodded.

There was a direct exit from the basement to the backyard, and as Jimmy was putting his shoes on, Gary approached him.

"You leaving?"

"Yeah, I gotta roll out. Meeting up with Sunny."

Gary didn't reply and instead just watched Jimmy finish putting on his shoes. Jimmy knew that Gary wanted to say something. Jimmy also knew that it wasn't anything he wanted to hear, so he didn't ask.

"I'll come out with you," Gary finally said. Jimmy shrugged. When they got outside, they saw Paul waiting as well by the house garage. Jimmy assumed he was waiting for his ride. The night was quiet as the three of them stood around. It was late December, but the winter so far had been tolerable. It had yet to snow, and the temperature was brisk but hadn't dropped to freezing.

Gary began talking to Paul about their upcoming basketball game, but Jimmy wasn't in the mood to participate in the conversation. Instead, he gazed around Mike's neighbourhood in Panorama Ridge. This was the "good" part of Surrey. The houses in the neighbourhood appeared more like mansions to Jimmy. He wouldn't have been surprised if two of his houses could fit into one of these. The yards were all landscaped with beautifully manicured gardens. He thought back to his own lawn, which hadn't been mown in months. Weeds even poked out of the cracks in the driveway.

Jessica didn't live far from Mike, and neither did Paul.

They could hear Sunny's car before seeing it. Jimmy knew Sunny was intentionally playing his music louder than usual. It wasn't long before the black-on-black Benz that had become synonymous with Sunny turned the corner and came into view.

It was chrome black, and it was always shining and spotless. The windows were tinted, so if you tried to look through to the inside, all you could see was your own reflection. It had a black leather interior and an incredible sound system. Jimmy loved that car.

Gary had met Sunny a few times before, so Sunny waved them both over when he pulled up to Mike's driveway. Ajay was sitting in the passenger seat, staring down at the cell phone in his lap, and didn't acknowledge them when they approached.

"Whatup, young bucks," Sunny hollered. "Y'all enjoying your kiddie party?"

They both managed a chuckle. "Yeah, it was bumpin'," Jimmy responded. "We're all pretty hammered."

"Doesn't look like that guy is having much fun," Sunny said, nodding his head in Paul's direction.

Jimmy turned around and saw Paul eyeing them with interest. His face was extremely serious. Jimmy wasn't even certain that Paul had been drinking at all. "He's whatever."

"What about you, big boy?" Sunny said to Gary.

Gary was large for a seventeen-year-old. Jimmy was six foot one but still had to look up at Gary, who was almost half a foot taller. Gary also weighed in at a cool 210 pounds, and he was strong and lean. Were it not for his baby face, he could easily have passed for a thirty-year-old, but he had soft, plump cheeks and still struggled to grow a moustache.

"I'm cool, man. What's up with you, Sunny?"

Sunny leaned back into his reclined chair. "You know me, man. Just doin' my thing. Makin' moves and makin' paper. What else is there?"

Gary nodded. "Yeah, I feel you."

"I'm about to get your boy making some *real* paper," Sunny continued. "We movin' up in the game. You let me know if you ever need work."

"Nah, he's straight," Jimmy interrupted. "He just came out to say whatup."

"That's cool. We cruising or what, Jimbo? Hop in."

Jimmy opened the back door and slid in. Ajay's and Sunny's seats were reclined so far back that they almost touched the back seats.

"I was actually gonna ask you if I can grab a dime bag," Gary said to Sunny.

Sunny laughed. "Sorry, brah, don't deal in those numbers no more. When it comes to the weed, you gotta buy an ounce to make it worth it. Let me know if you need anything else, though. White, Brown, M. Whatever you need. Tell your boys too."

Jimmy could feel himself clench up and his shoulders begin to get tight. Gary didn't need to know these things. Gary didn't say anything, and Jimmy could see his startled face before he nodded and walked away.

As they pulled out of the driveway, Jimmy looked back towards Mike's house and saw Paul watching them intently. Just before they turned the corner, Jimmy saw Paul wheel around and head back towards the basement.

– 2 –

"So whatup, youngin?" Sunny said.

Jimmy quickly shook off the irritation he was feeling. It was usually easier to forget things and let them be when you were high or drunk, as Jimmy had realized over the past year. Weed had become his substance of choice.

"Whatup, G? Whatup, Ajay? What's goin' on?"

Ajay grunted something Jimmy couldn't make out. Ajay looked and sounded like a bear. His gut hung almost to the glove department, and he was a heavy breather. He had the hairiest arms Jimmy had ever seen, but he still had decided to get full tattoo arm sleeves. His beard was thick and bushy, and he had a scar over his right eye. He didn't talk much. At least, not to Jimmy.

Jimmy knew instinctively that Sunny was working, and he was surprised Sunny had decided to bring out his Benz to work the shift. He had another beater of a car—an older Toyota Corolla that he usually drove when he was working. It was cheaper on gas—but more importantly, it drew much less attention.

There were two phones in the front console, and one of them was buzzing. Ajay answered with another grunt. "How much?... Where?... Be outside in five minutes. A hundred bucks." And then he hung up and mumbled something to Sunny, who simply nodded.

"So, you ready for this new chapter?" Sunny asked Jimmy.

Jimmy hesitated and felt a little off balance. *Must be the alcohol and weed.* He looked at the rear-view mirror and saw Sunny's eyes narrow as they focused on him and his reaction.

"Yeah, yeah, I'm ready, bro," Jimmy said quickly. "It's about time."

Sunny didn't reply and returned his attention to the road. Jimmy could see his eyes darting from side to side, scanning his surroundings.

"Cop," he said quietly to Ajay, giving a slight nod in the direction of about half a block up and to the right. Jimmy didn't see anything.

They kept their eyes to the front, but as they drove closer to where Sunny had nodded, Jimmy looked out the window. Sure enough, there was an undercover cop in a grey Dodge Charger, parked and on his laptop.

"How the hell did you see that cop from where we were?" Jimmy asked, stunned.

"Practice and attention," Sunny answered. "This is our livelihood. We don't mess around on these streets. This is business."

Jimmy had become accustomed to Sunny schooling him in the ways of the game, and he appreciated it. "If you treat the game right, the game will treat you right back," Sunny had told him. "All you gotta do is follow the rules." Sunny was tall and muscular and had a fresh fade, with a fresher beard. His clothes were fitted and always designer label.

"Where are we going?" Jimmy asked.

Ajay made his usual grunting noise, and Jimmy could see that he was hunched over a paper bag. He couldn't see what was in it, though.

"We gotta make a couple stops," said Sunny. "Pay attention, young blood. Do as we do."

The phone buzzed again, and Ajay answered with his signature grunt. "How much?... Where you at?... Be there in twenty."

Jimmy noticed how every phone call was kept brief. It was

like a challenge to see how few words you could say. Also, if Ajay said five minutes to be outside, it meant they were probably fifteen minutes away. They hated waiting. That was for their customers.

Eventually, Jimmy realized they were heading towards Whalley. If Panorama Ridge was the good part of Surrey, Whalley was the ghetto. A lot of the homeless and drug addicted congregated in the Whalley area. The streets were littered with lost souls just looking for their next high. The concentrated police presence in that area wasn't to stop them from using but to keep them alive. That's why Sunny told Jimmy to be on high alert whenever making a drop there.

"So how's life, little man?" Sunny asked. "Getting all your homework done on time?"

"Fuck school, man. Only reason I still go is so I can ball. We got a chance at making the provincials this year."

"That right, youngin?"

"Yeah. My teachers been on me, though. I've been slackin' with everything else."

"They don't want you winning, lil man. Anybody can be school smart; all you gotta do is memorize some numbers and places. But it's a cruel world out there. If you wanna survive, you gotta have your street smarts. That's the shit that sticks with you. You gotta learn how to read people. Read situations. Understand about makin' moves under pressure. And most important, learning how to stack some paper. With the money comes opportunity." Jimmy nodded before Sunny continued. "I know you're nervous about this shit. But it's necessary. Hustling dime bags barely pays for the gas and food. That's why I bought this line. They got a solid clientele. That's why Imma need you. There's gonna be too much money to go around. You feel me?"

"Yeah. You ain't nervous, though? About selling all this harder shit?"

Sunny didn't reply immediately. Jimmy could see his eyes continue scanning the road. They were almost in Whalley. "Different product, but the same game. We just gotta be more alert. More careful. Listen, lil bro. There are risks to this game. But there are risks to every game. I ain't saying I'm in this game forever. I'm gonna stack some paper, and maybe open me up a business or something."

Jimmy nodded again. He did notice, though, that maybe Sunny wasn't just trying to convince him. It seemed like he was trying to convince himself as well.

They turned onto King George Highway, which connected most of Surrey. They had taken side roads to get to this point. Sunny slowed up as he approached a cross street that was parallel to Surrey Memorial Hospital, which was probably the busiest hospital in all of BC. Sunny turned into a cul-de-sac, drove all the way to the end, and then parked the car on the side of the road. Jimmy could see someone waiting.

Sunny hung his arm casually out the window and waved in the person's direction. The guy began walking over, and as they got closer, Jimmy realized it was a boy not much older than he was. The boy had long, moppy hair that covered his forehead, and he wore jeans that looked like at any moment, they'd drop to the ground. His t-shirt was tattered, and Jimmy could see the skin of his chest.

As he approached the car, Jimmy saw his face and shuddered. His cheeks were hollow and narrow, with patches of peach-fuzz, and he was ghostly pale. From the streetlights, Jimmy could see that his arms were bony, and veins were popping along his forearms.

The boy approached the passenger side of Sunny's Benz, so it was Ajay he saw first. Jimmy could sense Ajay smile when he saw who the customer was.

"Hey," the boy said. Jimmy could hear the trembling undertones and knew the boy was nervous.

"You need an eight-ball, right?" Ajay said without looking up at the boy.

"Yeah."

"That's $150."

"What!? You said it was going to be $100 on the phone."

Ajay slowly looked at the boy. Jimmy couldn't see Ajay's face, but he did see the boy's expression, and he knew Ajay wasn't smiling anymore.

"$150."

"I only have $100 on me. That's what you said. Why isn't Jason working? Jason usually works at this time."

"Jason don't run this line no more. We do. $150. Take it or leave it."

"I told you, I only have $100 on me."

Ajay didn't say anything. Jimmy could hear him rustling with something in the front seat.

"You can't do that," Jimmy heard the boy say.

"You want it, yes or no? Should charge you more for wasting my time," Ajay said roughly.

Jimmy could tell the boy was fiending. He pulled out two crumpled fifty-dollar bills from his pocket and handed them to Ajay, who threw a plastic baggy of white powder on the pavement.

The car ride was silent as they made their way back. Jimmy could sense tension. Finally, Sunny pulled over to the side of the road and stared at Ajay. "What the hell was that?"

"What you mean?" Ajay replied.

"Don't give me that bullshit. This is my fuckin' business. That kid ain't never gonna call again."

Ajay turned to look at Sunny, and Jimmy could see his face was apologetic.

"My bad, man. I'm just a little on edge. I just needed a little something to get me through."

Jimmy now realized that Ajay had taken some of the cocaine out of the kid's baggie.

"You got a problem, man. You better take care of it," Sunny said to Ajay.

"I know, I know."

Sunny stared ahead and Jimmy knew he was thinking. "Well go ahead, then. Bust the rail," he finally said.

Jimmy saw Ajay lean over and heard a snorting noise.

Ajay shook his head quickly as if the drug had reenergized him.

"You want some?" Ajay asked Sunny.

"You know I don't do that shit when I'm working. Give it to the kid. You ever try a little white, lil man?"

"Nah. I'm straight, though. I'm still buzzin' off vodka. I'm chillin'."

Sunny turned around and looked at Jimmy with a mischievous grin. "How you gonna sell this shit if you ain't never tried it? Don't go soft on me now, boy."

Sunny pulled a twenty-dollar bill out of his pocket and rolled it into a short, tight cylinder with a hole at each end. Without asking Jimmy again, he nodded at Ajay, who handed Jimmy the insurance papers he had pulled from the glove compartment. There was a long, white line of powder in the middle of the paper.

Jimmy had never even considered doing cocaine. He had only

ever even seen the white powder for the first time last week when Sunny had picked up the product. He had helped him bag it up.

In the rear-view mirror, Jimmy could see Sunny's eyes narrow again. The white line was staring up at Jimmy, almost daring him. Jimmy felt his heart begin to race, and he knew there was nowhere to run or hide. It didn't really feel like he had a choice.

Jimmy placed the tip of the cylinder at one end of the line, then put his nostril to the other end and sniffed deeply as he moved down the line until he had snorted all the powder.

He was surprised at how quickly he felt the rush of euphoria pulsate through his body. There was a numbing sensation in his nose, but the excitement of the drug drowned it out. Jimmy sensed his heart begin to beat faster. He felt intensely more alert and awake, then a surge of confidence coupled with an underlying sense of calm. He was still drunk, but it was like the alcohol took a backseat to this new drug.

"How you feel?" Sunny asked.

"G-o-o-d." And he meant it.

Sunny laughed as he pulled away from the curb and headed to their next call.

~ 3 ~

Jimmy stared absent-mindedly at the passage he was supposed to be reading.

"So what do you think is the underlying theme?" Jessica asked.

Without immediately responding, Jimmy tried harder to focus. But he couldn't. It just looked like gibberish to him. He leaned back into his chair. "What's the point of this, anyways?" he asked coolly.

Jessica gave him an exasperated look. "Jimmy, you have to finish the assignment."

"I know. But what's the point?" he asked her again. "Like, I really don't get what this has to do with anything."

"I don't know. Getting a decent education so you can do something with your life? If you want to play basketball in college, you're going to have to be able to do assignments like this."

He shrugged, then glared again at the pages. It was a passage from *Hamlet*. "When was this written again? Like, 500 years ago, right? You would think they'd be able to find something better for us to read since then. Who even speaks like this?"

Jessica gave Jimmy a sarcastic smile as she shook her head. "Does it really matter? This assignment was due last week. Ms. Chohan isn't going to let you put it off much longer."

This was the answer Jimmy had come to expect. Anytime he would question someone about the purpose of what he thought of as pointless assignments, they couldn't give him a straight answer. Instead, they'd avoid the question and tell him that's just the way things were.

Jimmy swivelled his neck from side to side and stretched his arms above his head.

Jessica just looked at him with a blank expression. He always made things so difficult for her. "Do you not understand it? I can help you with that," she said.

"Do you want to help?" Jimmy asked coyly.

"Of course. What can I do?"

"Let's go upstairs to your room. I'll come back all refreshed and ready to study."

"Hahaha, you're too much."

Jimmy playfully nudged her leg. Jessica was gorgeous. She had long, thick, black hair, piercing hazel eyes, and dimples when she smiled. Her body was mature for her age. She had curves in all the right places, and Jimmy couldn't help but undress her with his eyes in that moment. She was a high-school boy's dream, and she was Jimmy's girl.

"Come on," he prodded.

"I can't, Jimmy. My parents are home. You know my parents don't let me close the door when you're over."

It was Jimmy's turn to laugh. "Oh yeah, I forgot about that. We know how your parents feel about me."

Jessica looked away. "It's not like that, Jimmy," she finally said. "They're just overprotective. They just want the best for me." Instantly, she regretted saying this as she felt Jimmy glaring at her.

"What does that mean? They don't think I'm good enough for you?" Jimmy shut his book. "I gotta go anyways. I'll talk to you later."

Jimmy was putting his book into his backpack when he felt Jessica's hand reach forward and touch his. The softness of her hands always sent vibrations through his body. No matter how he was feeling, her touch could always calm him down.

"I'm sorry," she said softly. "But we both know you've been on edge lately. And I know it's more than just basketball playoffs coming up. Why won't you talk to me about it? I want to be here for you."

Jimmy looked up from his backpack, and his gaze met hers. In that moment he wanted to tell her everything. He wanted to be relieved of the burden on his shoulders. But he couldn't. He refused to accept that he wasn't doing the right thing, and he knew Jessica would try to convince him otherwise, so he remained silent.

"Do you know what I just found?" Jessica asked when she accepted Jimmy wasn't going to say anything. Jimmy shook his head. She stood up and left the room without saying a word, returning a few moments later. She had a photo in her hand, and she handed it to Jimmy.

Jimmy grinned. It was a class photo of their grade seven year at Beaver Creek Elementary. He looked at all the smiling faces of his classmates and remembered a time that seemed so much simpler. In the back row, smiles plastered on their faces, stood Jimmy and Gary with their arms around each other's shoulders.

"Wow." Jimmy continued to stare at the picture, recalling how close he and Gary had gotten that year. That was the year Gary's dad had left their family.

Jimmy then found Jessica in the picture. She was sitting on a bench right in front, hands placed neatly in her lap. Her posture was very impressive for a twelve-year-old kid. Her hair was short, and she wore a baggy sweater. But what Jimmy noticed the most was her smile, which took up nearly her entire face. Jimmy had forgotten that she had worn braces that year.

"Wow, you were an awkward looking kid," Jimmy chuckled.

She laughed as she punched him playfully on the arm.

Jimmy looked back down at the picture and felt a warmth inside that sometimes he forgot was there. "Those were good times."

"Yeah, they were. But these are good times too." She sat on Jimmy's lap. "I had my first kiss that year," she said, pointing to the picture.

Jimmy smiled. "Me too. I think you cut me with your braces."

Jessica laughed. "Well you would have deserved it. I don't think you said a word to me for about three years after. Maybe you just wanted to brag to your friends."

Jimmy squeezed her sides gently. "You know it wasn't like that. We were just kids. I didn't know what the hell to do. And look, we found our way back in the end."

Jessica nodded as she looked out her bedroom window, reminiscing. "I still remember the day you asked me out. Last year at the winter dance. You were so sweet and charming. You told me that you thought I looked beautiful. And you told me that you still remembered our first kiss and how awkward but amazing it was. And then you asked me to dance. I still think about that night."

Jimmy smiled. "It was an amazing night, wasn't it," he said. "We had our second kiss together that night."

Jessica smiled, but this time he couldn't help but notice the sadness in her eyes.

"What's up?" Jimmy asked.

Jessica hesitated before replying. "Things have just been different lately. I guess I just miss those times when we first started hanging out and I was the only person you wanted to hang out with. And with Sunny… People have been telling me the types of things he's involved in. And I know you know what people have been saying."

Jimmy felt his stomach muscles tighten. "People can say what they wanna say, but in reality, they don't know anything about him. Sunny keeps it real in a world where it's so easy to be fake. And he's been there for me, and you know that. All we do is blaze together. I promise."

"You know I don't care that you blaze. But you've just been doing it so much. It's like you're trying to escape from something. You see the world in a different way than anybody else I know. It's like sometimes you see right through it. And that's what I love about you. But it's also what worries me the most."

Jimmy could see the love radiating from Jessica's eyes, and he wanted her to be okay. He didn't want her to hurt over him. "I'm going to be fine," he said softly. "Just give me a little time to figure some things out." Then he stood them both up. "But I do have to head out. I'll finish up the assignment at home." He flung his backpack over his shoulder and gave Jessica a peck on the lips. "I'll see you at school."

– 4 –

Jimmy left Jessica's house but didn't feel like going home. Instead, he sat in his car for a few minutes, gazing out the window. The rain that had been pouring down when he had arrived at Jessica's had stopped, and now the sun was peeking through the clouds.

He didn't want to be alone, so he pulled out his phone and dialled Gary's number.

"Whatup, bro?" Jimmy said when Gary answered.

"Chillin' just at the mall. What you up to?"

"Nothing, man. Bored. Wanna chill?"

"Yeah, I'm down. Where you want to meet?"

"Let's meet up at the cage," Jimmy said.

"Aight, cool. I'll be there in, like, half an hour."

Jimmy hung up and massaged his shoulders before starting the car. His shoulders and especially his neck had been bothering him for the past few months. No matter how much he massaged or stretched them, he couldn't relieve the tension that seemed to have made a permanent home there.

Jimmy pulled up to the cage and turned his car off, looking out at the basketball court where he had first learned to love the game.

The cage had become Jimmy's second home over the past ten years. He would go there when nothing else seemed to make sense and he needed somewhere to get away. Kids in the area would call it the cage because of the chain-link fence that surrounded the full-sized basketball court. It was cement ground, with painted white lines. On either side were two basketball hoops with white backboards and red trim. The hoops had chain nets that would make a rattling sound when you swished your jump shot. Surrounding the cage were several tall trees that blocked out the visual of one of the busiest streets in Surrey. You couldn't see the hundreds of cars that would drive by every hour, but you could still hear them.

He reflected on a day just under a year ago, when he'd first met Sunny...

It had been a cold, brisk evening when Jimmy stormed out. The cage was only a five-minute walk from his house, and he was glad to find it empty. He had lashed out at his dad while his mom silently prepared dinner, tears swimming in her eyes.

Jimmy's basketball shoes had ripped halfway through the season, and his parents had promised to buy him new ones. But months had passed, and it was always the same goddamn excuse about not having enough money and just waiting a few more weeks. Jimmy was so tired of being poor. And what made him even angrier was the lack of reaction he got from his dad, who just looked at the ground, embarrassed by the insults Jimmy was pelting him with.

While other kids in his grade were coming to school in their new Jordans and Nike tracksuits, Jimmy's wardrobe was full of oversized clothes that his mom found at thrift stores.

He pounded the ball on the asphalt before swishing another jump shot. As he walked to collect the ball, a black Benz screeched into the parking lot. Rap music was blasting through the tinted windows as it pulled up to the cage. The volume dropped, and he could see someone in the driver's seat talking on the phone. Jimmy did his best to ignore the visitor as he swished another jump shot.

Eventually, the door opened, and out stepped Sunny. He was tall, muscular and had full tattoo sleeves on both arms. Despite the temperature, he wore a black fitted t-shirt over bulging pecs and biceps.

On his feet were the freshest pair of Jordan's Jimmy had ever seen.

"Sup, young buck," Sunny said to him.

Jimmy felt his heartbeat instantly increase but remained cool. "Not much. Just shooting some hoops. Getting ready for a game tomorrow. Nice kicks. Those the new Jordan's?"

"Ah shit, you like your J's too, huh?" Sunny replied, opening the cage door and stepping inside. "I used to be a baller back in the day too. Pass the ball here, son. Let me get one up."

Jimmy tossed him the ball.

Sunny took a few dribbles, then threw an awkward jump shot that completely missed the hoop.

"Haaa, bit rusty. Let me throw up one more."

Jimmy collected the ball and passed it back to him.

Sunny glanced down and noticed Jimmy's shoes. "Whatup with your kicks, son?"

Jimmy looked down at his feeble attempt to keep his shoes together with duct tape. He'd had this pair since grade nine, and his toes were jammed all the way to the front from growing.

"Haha, yeah. I'm getting new ones soon. Just making do with what I got for now, I guess. I'm still ballin' out like nobody's business."

Sunny smiled and then paused briefly as if contemplating something.

"You blaze, young buck?" he asked.

Jimmy shook his head. "Not really. I've done it a few times with my buddies. But it doesn't do much for me."

Sunny smiled before producing the fattest joint that Jimmy had ever seen.

"OG kush brah. This shit will solve all your problems."

From his other pocket, he pulled out a lighter and sparked the joint. He took a few deep inhales before passing the joint to Jimmy.

Jimmy hesitated for the briefest moment before accepting the joint and taking a hit himself. The smoke smacked his lungs hard, and before he knew it, he was doubled over, coughing.

Sunny laughed. "Still a lightweight. All good, young buck. You got fresh lungs. This is the most killz shit that you're gonna find anywhere. Believe that."

Jimmy nodded as he managed to stand upright, somewhat embarrassed. He could already feel the effects of the weed in his head.

"So what school you go to?" Sunny asked.

"Tamanawis," Jimmy answered nodding his head towards his high school, which could be seen from the cage.

"Ahh shit... Tammy... That's where I went. That foo Dhillon still there? Tell him Sunny says whatup."

Jimmy nodded, making no mental note to ever deliver the message.

Sunny looked back down at Jimmy's shoes and chuckled again. "Imma do something for you, youngin'. Out of the kindness of my heart. I don't want Tammy boys walking around rockin' shoes like that."

He pulled out a wad of cash from his pocket, slipped out two one-hundred-dollar bills, and offered them to Jimmy.

Jimmy shook his head. "I'm good, man. My parents taking me shopping tomorrow. I appreciate it, though."

Sunny laughed again. "I insist, brah. This is nothing to me.

I'm always giving back to my community. Makes me feel all fuzzy inside."

Jimmy looked again at the money, then at Sunny's black Benz, then back at Sunny, who was just smiling. Damn, he did need new shoes.

Jimmy put his hand out and took the cash. "Thanks, man. Really appreciate it."

"No sweat, young buck. I gotta jet, though. I'll see you around. Maybe I'll stop by one of your games and say whatup."

Jimmy sat in his car, thinking back to that moment when he had accepted the two hundred-dollar bills. He had finally been able to replace his old, duct-taped Reebok's with fresh Jordan's, and he could still remember the excitement bubbling in his stomach when he'd handed the cashier the money for his shoes and when he'd first tried them on at home. He'd even had enough money left over to get a fresh cut and a beard trimming at the barber. He loved the feeling of looking good.

It was during that summer going into his grade twelve year that he and Sunny had begun to get close. At first, Sunny would show up randomly to the cage, and if Jimmy was there, which he usually was, they would smoke a joint. It wasn't long before Jimmy started to want to get high more often, and it would be him initiating the phone call. The weed was the only thing that seemed to quiet his mind, which would not or could not be shut off.

By the end of the summer, Sunny would sell Jimmy a couple of ounces at a time at a really good price. Jimmy would then sell some to his buddies for pocket money and smoke the rest.

Jessica found out pretty quickly.

"It's just weed," Jimmy had told her. "I don't sell it. I just have it on me. And if my boys want some, what's the harm in me being the source? They're gonna get it somewhere else anyways."

Eventually, he'd built up a handful of carefully picked clients of his own. It was the perfect amount to make sure he always had a few bucks in his pocket but word wouldn't spread about what he was doing. And from time to time, he would work Sunny's line phone, when it was just weed that Sunny was selling.

Things had changed a lot over the past couple of months, though. Sunny had bought an established line from another drug dealer who sold pretty much everything. Sunny and Ajay could only work it so much, and that was when Sunny had "asked" Jimmy...

The sun had emerged from the clouds and was shining down on the cage, interrupting Jimmy's reverie. He got out of his car and opened the trunk, where he always kept a basketball. Walking into the cage, he caressed the smooth leather of his basketball as lovingly as a mother would stroke her baby's forehead. The early evening air had a fresh fragrance that was always present after a long rainfall. Jimmy took a deep inhale, letting the air fill his lungs.

Slowly, he walked up to the three-point line. He dribbled twice with his right hand, and then rose up, letting the ball soar off his fingertips. He felt the rotation of the ball, saw the high arc of the shot, and knew it was a swish. As he collected the ball, he heard another car pull up to the cage.

Jimmy's five-year-old Honda Civic looked like a Bentley compared to Gary's beater of a car, which appeared to be a ride away from breaking down.

Gary stepped out of his car and gave Jimmy the customary goofy smile Jimmy had grown to love. He trudged over to the cage and had to finagle the latch before he got it open.

"Hey, Jimmy."

"Whatup, G," Jimmy replied, throwing him the ball.

Gary took two awkward dribbles from the three-point line and threw up a shot that barely grazed the rim.

"You tired from the game yesterday?" Gary asked, collecting the ball and passing it to Jimmy. "You had to carry us on your back. Again."

Jimmy laughed. "Nah. I could go out and play another one today." He had carried Tamanawis to a twenty-four-point victory yesterday against Enver Creek, piling in thirty-four points even though he had sat out the fourth quarter. They had only one more regular season game, against Guildford Park Secondary, who was in last place before playoffs started.

Gary was the starting center, and he was a menacing presence in the paint. Although not coordinated, he was big and strong. Despite being able to jump less than a foot off the ground, he could still out-rebound most players on the court. And he set hard, solid screens that would send defenders flying backwards. Most of all, he was the enforcer that Jimmy needed to keep the defense honest. If the opposing team delivered a dirty foul or a cheap shot to Jimmy, they knew they would have to answer to Gary.

"How was the mall?" Jimmy asked.

"It was chill, man. Mike and me went. My broke ass can't afford shit. But I munched two Quizno footlongs." He laughed. "Hit the gym earlier, so I was hungry."

"Damn, I gotta get back into the weights too. Get my weight up a bit." Jimmy was lean, but he was naturally strong. Despite his more athletic build, he always challenged himself to keep up with the weights that Gary was lifting.

"What you get up to?" Gary asked. "Chillin' with Jessica?"

"Yeah, she was trying to get me to do some lame-ass book report or something."

"Could be worse," Gary said. "At least she's trying to help."

"Yeah, I guess," Jimmy shrugged.
"You get it in or what?"
"Tried. But you know Jess. She's all up on me about school. It can get exhausting sometimes. And she's always trying to bring up Sunny these days."
Gary started to say something but then stopped mid-sentence.
"What?" Jimmy said. "What were you going to say?"
"Nothing, forget it."
"Tell me," Jimmy said, more demandingly this time.
Gary hesitated before answering. "Well, she might be right. You've been slackin' at school lately. And it isn't like you couldn't breeze through your classes if you wanted to. Two things I know about you, Jimbo. You're the best baller I know. And you're smarter than what you give yourself credit for. And what was Sunny talking about last weekend? About moving up in the game and not dealing dime bags no more?"
Jimmy caressed the ball, enjoying the leathery texture and how it made his fingertips tingle. "Sunny bought a line. Hustling White, Brown, M, all of it."
"What? You serious?"
"Yeah, and he asked me to help him work the line."
"You ain't thinking about it, are you? That's insane."
Jimmy glared at Gary. "Of all people, you should know why I'm doin' what I'm doin'."
"Damn man, I just don't want nothing to happen to you. You can go somewhere in ball if you want to. And I know you're tired of people telling you that. But it's true. You just gotta get your school shit done."
"You wanna know what I think about school?" Jimmy asked Gary.
"What?"

"It makes sense for people who want to grow up and have that nine-to-five job. It's for those people who wanna grind their whole lives for some goddamn pension that they won't get until they're impotent and halfway in the dirt. What the fuck do I want that for? And you know what else? Anytime I ask somebody what the point is in getting an education, they can't even give me a straight answer. Nah, man, that's not what life is about." All of a sudden, Jimmy felt hot. People would talk to him about getting a college education like it was something that he even wanted, and that made him angry.

"So what do you think life is about then?"

Jimmy paused. He had been pondering this question a lot more lately. He knew what he *didn't* want. But he still hadn't figured out what he did.

"I'll tell you this much, bro. Money makes this world go round. Look at Sunny. He ain't got no college education, but he drives a nicer ride than any teacher at Tammy. He's got this game figured out."

Gary didn't say anything. He had a pained expression on his face, and Jimmy knew he was holding back. Gary was his best friend, and his oldest friend.

Jimmy heard his phone vibrating in his pocket. He pulled it out and saw that it was a text from Sunny: "U working the evening shift on Sunday."

Jimmy felt his heart begin to beat more rapidly as he put the phone back into his pocket. He reached into his other pocket and pulled out a joint. "Perks of being a hustler. Down to blaze?" he asked.

Gary had that goofy grin on his face that Jimmy loved as he nodded.

~ 5 ~

SUNDAY NIGHT HAD arrived as Jimmy sat on the desk chair in his bedroom, staring mindlessly at his backpack. He still hadn't completed the assignment that he'd promised Jess that he would do. His mind was elsewhere, racing with what he had to get done tonight. He unzipped the bottom compartment of his backpack and pulled out a Ziploc bag containing a half dozen joints. Pulling one out, he stood up from his chair and walked to his half-open window. He pushed it open further and leaned his head out. From here, he had a clear view of his old elementary school and a life that sometimes he wished he could return to.

He sparked the joint and felt better before he had even taken the first puff. His heartbeat began to slow, and the familiar unease in the pit of his stomach lessened. The first drag was slow and deliberate, as he allowed the THC to enter his bloodstream.

Jimmy gazed lovingly at the joint in his hand as the smoke drifted off the tip. This was the only medication that he would ever need—contrary to what the doctors used to tell him when he was a child.

It had started when Jimmy was in grade six, at the same elementary school that he was now looking at.

He was sitting in class, listening to his teacher, Mr. Katz, when he first felt it. His chair began to feel unstable, and he suddenly had a fear that it was going to topple over. He grasped the sides of his desk, which steadied him for a moment and allowed him to survey the classroom. Everything felt like it was shifting off balance, almost as if there was an earthquake. Except his classmates continued gazing blandly up at Mr. Katz.

He began to feel nauseous, like he was going to vomit. The lights from above invaded his eyes, and his head began to throb. He closed his eyes, hoping that would help, but it only made things worse. He began to panic and he stood up, trying to excuse himself to go to the washroom, but it felt like the floor was moving from under him.

Right when he felt like he was going to faint, someone put their hand on his back, and Jimmy leaned against them. The person led Jimmy outside to the hallway, and Jimmy heard the person muttering something to the teacher as they left.

The person guided Jimmy to a side hallway door that led outside. It was a chilly afternoon, and the cold breeze instantly made Jimmy feel a bit better. He looked up and saw it was Gary who had helped him. Jimmy allowed Gary to lead him to a bench, where they both sat down. Jimmy hung his head towards the pavement as Gary sat in silence.

That was the first episode of several to happen throughout the following few years. They would come without warning, and the more they happened, the more fragile and vulnerable Jimmy had begun to feel.

He visited a multitude of doctors over the next few years, and he couldn't even count how many tests he underwent. He began to tune out, sitting expressionless while doctors explained to him that everything seemed perfectly normal on all of the tests. His parents, and especially his mom, held on to hope that eventually a doctor would find something, and he would be cured. He knew how much his mom was hurting, knowing she could do nothing for her son.

Jimmy remembered one doctor. Dr. Foti was his name, and he was a neurologist. He was a short, stocky man with a pencil-thin moustache clinging to his upper lip. He was balding but still sported a comb-over with a few wispy strands of hair. He walked with an air of arrogance, and his office wall was full of certificates boasting his degrees and accreditations.

Jimmy recalled Dr. Foti sitting him and his parents down and uttering so many diagnoses that Jimmy couldn't even keep up. He spat out words like "anxiety, depression, migraines, antidepressants," as if he had said them to a thousand patients before.

Jimmy could still vividly remember how he'd felt as he stared at this doctor who was trying to convince his parents what was wrong with him. His voice was monotonous and dull, and Jimmy had the strongest urge to tell the doctor what *he* thought was wrong with *him*.

To appease his parents, Jimmy popped some pills that Dr. Foti prescribed. He even held on to a silent hope that maybe these would "cure" him. After a few months of taking the medication, Jimmy began to feel deadened and emotionless, like there was a haze hanging around his entire life. Nothing seemed to matter anymore. It wasn't long before he flushed the pills down his toilet.

Eventually, the nausea and migraines mainly stopped, but something else took its place—a chronic tension-type feeling that radiated from his traps, up through his neck and around his forehead. It was like there was a band wrapped around his head that was constantly being squeezed. There was only one thing that Jimmy could count on to relieve the tension: the joint in his hand.

Jimmy took one final, deep toke as he allowed the night breeze to brush up against his face. He swallowed the smoke in his mouth down into his lungs and held it there. Closing his eyes, he felt the effects of the weed course through his body. He opened his eyes and exhaled, admiring the contrast of the smoke against the darkness of the night.

From downstairs, he could faintly hear his mom try to wake up his dad for his evening shift. His dad drove a taxi during the day and worked as a cleaner in the evening. He had been working two jobs for as long as Jimmy could remember. Jimmy might stumble into him once every few days, but other than that, their relationship was non-existent. It was like they were strangers living in the same home.

Jimmy's parents had both emigrated from India in their late teens and had lived in Surrey ever since. They were gentle, unassuming people who did their best to create a modest life in Canada. They had a handful of friends, and their lives were predicated on habit and pattern. They had never been able to get over the unfamiliarity of being in a new country, and they had become meek and timid.

Jimmy could hear the front door close, and he knew his dad had left. Jimmy walked downstairs and could hear his mom cleaning up in the kitchen. She heard him and called out: "Jimmy, would you like any dinner? Roti and daal?"

"No, I'm good," Jimmy replied.

"Are you sure? I made plenty."

"I said I'm good." This time, his voice was rude. Jimmy looked towards the living room, which was to the left of the kitchen. He could see the Crown Royal bottle in its usual spot in the middle of the coffee table. His dad had left his empty glass beside it and his half-eaten plate of dinner for his mom to clean up.

Jimmy slipped on his Jordan's, which were pushed up against the wall by the front door.

"What time are you going to be home?" his mom asked as she stood at the entrance of the kitchen.

"I'm not sure. Not till late, probably. Don't wait up," Jimmy answered.

"You have school tomorrow."

Jimmy offered her half a nod before he opened the door and walked outside into the crisp January evening.

His car was parked about half a kilometer up the street from their house, as Sunny had told him to do. Jimmy didn't understand exactly why, and Sunny didn't like being questioned.

Jimmy approached his smoke-grey Honda Civic and pulled the keys from his pocket. Fifteen minutes later, he was in front of Sunny's house. Sunny lived in a basement in a somewhat secluded neighbourhood of Surrey, still in the process of being developed. Only a handful of houses had been built in a cul-de-sac that could probably fit more than two dozen by the time it was completed. Scattered throughout the street were half-built houses, along with wood and other construction materials. By this time, the workers had gone home, leaving the night eerily silent.

He saw Sunny's black Benz parked on the road, fresh from the car wash. Just behind it was a navy-blue, older-model Lexus that belonged to Ajay. A half block down was the Toyota Corolla that Sunny would usually drive when he was working.

Jimmy walked along the side of the house and knocked on Sunny's door.

"Who is it?" a deep voice asked. Sunny and Ajay knew he was coming, but they weren't the trusting types.

"It's Jimmy."

The door opened, and Jimmy was met by Ajay's ever-present menacing stare. His gut was hanging through his shirt, but his massive chest and broad shoulders were definitely intimidating. Jimmy knew that Ajay did a ton of steroids, and to his credit, he did spend a lot of time in the gym, but his diet consisted of fast food and pop.

Jimmy stepped in and was greeted by the smell of stale smoke and a bin of trash that seemed to be decaying in the corner. Ajay sat back down at a small, round kitchen table, where he was in the middle of rolling a fat blunt. Beside the pile of weed that he was rolling from was an ashtray full of at least a dozen smoked blunts and joints. Jimmy wouldn't have been surprised if they were all from today.

Loud music was blaring in the background. Jimmy loved rap, but this was trap music, and it was all Sunny and Ajay would play. Jimmy had tried to get into it, but he couldn't. None of the songs had any substance. To Jimmy, it just sounded like gibberish.

Sunny was laid up on the couch, playing NBA 2K. He was yelling at the TV. "Fuckin' Lebron. This shit is unrealistic. He always dunks that shit." He looked up at Jimmy. "Whatup, young buck," he said, putting the game on pause. "Always on time. I like that. Unlike some people," he said, motioning towards Ajay. "You gotta learn from the young buck, Ajay. The boy's got initiative."

Ajay grunted as he lit the blunt, then passed it to Sunny, who took a few deep tokes as he stared at Jimmy.

"You nervous about tonight?" he asked.

Jimmy shook his head, although his heart rate indicated otherwise.

Sunny surveyed him intently and then smiled. "I'm proud of you, little man. You've come a long way since we first met. I know you got a handle on these streets. That's why I'm trustin' you with this."

"I appreciate that, big bro."

Sunny passed Jimmy the blunt, and he inhaled deeply, then exhaled the cloud of smoke into the room. Jimmy had never asked Sunny about the people living upstairs. They didn't seem like a concern to him.

Sunny stood up. "Follow me, little man." Sunny led Jimmy through a narrow hallway that connected to his bedroom. Once they were there, Sunny closed the door. Jimmy hadn't been inside Sunny's room before. Clothes were scattered on the floor, and there were empty cans of pop sitting on his dresser. He had a king-size bed with a massive frame, which fit well in the surprisingly large space.

Sunny walked over to a corner of the room, bent down, and began to turn the combination lock of a fairly large safe. He pulled out a brown paper bag, then stood up to face Jimmy. "I know you're hesitant about this shit." Jimmy began to tell him that he wasn't, but Sunny interrupted. "You ain't gotta front with me. Shit, I'm a little nervous too, but I bought this line so we can take that next step and see some real paper. Hustling dime bags just ain't cuttin' it no more. If we're in this game, we gotta do it right. We gotta bleed this shit dry. Don't even worry 'bout the shit you're selling. It's the same game, just a different clientele."

Jimmy nodded. He wanted to say something, but his mouth had gone dry.

"Everything's ready to go. Product is all measured and bagged up," Sunny continued. He handed a cell phone and the brown paper bag to Jimmy. "You hit me up if anything pops up."

"Of course, bro."

− 6 −

It was a perfectly clear night as Jimmy drove down 64th Avenue, a street he had gotten to know very well over the years. After all, he just lived two blocks over on 66th Avenue. Sixty-fourth connected most of Surrey and led all the way out to Langley and Abbotsford if you drove far enough. In the other direction, it led you onto a highway that could take you to pretty much any other city in the Lower Mainland.

Jimmy heard the phone vibrate on the seat next to him. He scanned the road for any police, then picked it up. "Hello," he said in a voice deeper than his natural one.

"Hey," a trembling voice stuttered on the other side. "Umm… I need… some smack… uhhh…. some brown sugar."

"How much?" Jimmy replied impatiently.

"I dunno. Like, two or three hits. How much?"

"Forty bucks. What's your address?" The guy managed to spit out the name of a bar. "Ten minutes. Be outside," Jimmy said, then hung up.

He reached into his glove department and pulled out the heroin, already sorted into small plastic bags. It felt weird pulling out brown powder rather than the green herb he had become accustomed to seeing.

He took a left onto King George Highway and headed towards the shadier part of Surrey, pulling up to a sleazy pub in Whalley called The Snakepit about twenty minutes later. Jimmy glanced around the parking lot and didn't see anybody standing outside. He could feel his blood begin to boil and his mind act up. Like Sunny, Jimmy hadn't mastered the virtue of patience. He picked up the phone and dialled the number that had called earlier. Before it went to a second ring, he saw the front door of The Snakepit open. Out stumbled a Caucasian man in his late fifties. He had a white, patchy beard and wispy white hair. Clinging to his arm was a female who looked to be in her late thirties. She was wearing a black leather skirt that was hiked up halfway past her knees, and a white see-through blouse that showed big, sagging boobs. Layers of makeup couldn't hide her wrinkled face and sunken eyes. Her skin was flabby and loose. Jimmy looked at them half in disgust and half in pity.

They spotted his Honda Civic, and the man approached it cautiously. Jimmy put his hand up, motioning for him to go to the passenger-side window, which Jimmy lowered to halfway. "You got the cash?" he asked the man, who was old enough to be his father.

The man nodded nervously. His hands were trembling as he reached into his pocket and fished out two crumpled twenty-dollar bills. He handed them over to Jimmy, who pocketed them then reached into the front cup holder, where he had put the heroin, and handed it to the man.

The man's eyes immediately lit up, and he accepted it gratefully. "Thank you, thank you."

Jimmy nodded, shutting the window and pulling out of the parking lot. From his rear-view mirror, Jimmy could see the woman hugging the man. *Fuckin' fiends,* he thought.

His phone buzzed again, and he took a quick look at his surroundings, then answered in his gruff voice.

A clear, crisp voice responded, catching Jimmy off guard. "Hello, where abouts are you right now?" the voice asked.

"On the road. Where you at and what you need?"

"I'm in a hotel in Delta and need an eight ball. I need it asap. How long?"

"I'll be there in ten minutes. It's gonna run you $120."

"Okay," the man said.

After getting the man's address, Jimmy hung up and made a right turn. It was nearing midnight, and the roads were mainly deserted. Jimmy drove down Nordel Road, which at peak time was congested bumper to bumper. But at this time, Jimmy was cruising, seeming to hit every green light. He tried to relax his tensed-up shoulders as he changed the song on his sound system. "Me Against the World" by 2pac began to play, and Jimmy reclined deeper into his seat, letting the music consume him. If you asked Jimmy who his role models were, he wouldn't tell you his parents or any of his teachers. He would tell you 2pac, Nipsey Hussle, and maybe even Sunny. They spoke the rules of the game in a way that he could actually understand. All three shared one thing in common: they had spent their adolescent years hustling on the streets, making money so they had options when they got older. Jimmy could hear thoughts begin to circulate through his mind as the music played in the background.

He pulled up to a hotel called the Delta Rise. Jimmy stared up at the building, and it seemed to stretch upwards forever into the dark sky. There was not a cloud in sight, and everything seemed still and quiet.

Jimmy could see a gentleman in an impressive three-piece suit standing in the lobby, looking directly at him. Jimmy saw him reach into his pocket and pull out his phone. Jimmy's vibrated from the passenger seat, and he answered it.

"Is that you?" the voice on the other line asked. "In the grey Honda Civic?"

"Yeah," Jimmy replied. He could see the man hang up the phone and open the door to the hotel.

The guy was tall, over six foot three, and he had a slim but solid build, short blonde hair, and a strong jaw. As he walked closer, Jimmy could see the man looking at him out of deep blue eyes. It flitted through Jimmy's head that he could have been a model for Calvin Klein.

Jimmy lowered his window.

"Nice digs," Jimmy said, nodding at the man's suit.

"Thanks." He reached into his pocket and pulled out a wad of cash held together by one of those money clips that Jimmy would see at Gucci stores. The man slipped off a brown note and a green one and handed them to Jimmy, who reached into the front cup holder and passed him the plastic baggie of cocaine.

When Jimmy turned to hand it over, their eyes met. Now that the man was only a few feet away, Jimmy saw someone different. His eyes were bloodshot, with dark brown bags underneath, as if he hadn't slept in days. One corner of the man's mouth twitched as if he had lost control of some of his voluntary movements. The man's lips were chapped, and there was drool hanging from the side of his mouth.

Jimmy handed him the cocaine, and the man gave Jimmy a brief nod before turning and heading back inside. Jimmy smirked as he pulled out of the Delta Rise parking lot. *Dope fiends aren't just in Whalley.*

By the end of his shift, it was nearly 4 a.m., and Jimmy's eyes were drooping. He struggled to keep them open as he pulled into a McDonald's drive-through.

"What can I get for you," said the voice from the drive-through speaker. It had a thick Indian accent.

"Uhhh… Get me two juniors and a dozen nuggets."

"Nine dollars. First window, please."

Jimmy pulled up to the window and was nearly falling asleep when a voice called out, "Jimmy! Is that you?"

His eyes shot open as he looked to the drive-through window. Standing there with a gigantic smile was Karnbir. Karnbir had emigrated from India at the start of their grade eight year. When he had first come to Tamanawis, he could not speak a word of English. But he was persistent in learning, and with his joyful attitude, he had made plenty of friends. Jimmy couldn't remember a time when he hadn't seen Karnbir smiling.

"Hey, Karnbir," Jimmy said sleepily. "I didn't know you worked here."

Karnbir nodded. "4 a.m. to 8 a.m. It's not too bad. And my parents can use the help. How about you? What are you doing here so early?"

"Uhhh… Just a late night. Hung out with some of the boys. You know how it is."

Karnbir laughed. "Not really."

Jimmy smiled. "We'll invite you out one time. Give you a night to remember." He reached into his pocket and handed Karnbir a ten-dollar bill.

Karnbir took a quick peek behind him, then shrugged the bill off. "Don't worry about it," he said with a wink.

"Thanks, buddy. See you at school."

After Jimmy had dropped the stuff back off with Sunny, he finally pulled up to his usual spot about half a kilometer away from his house. It was still dark outside, but Jimmy knew that it wouldn't be long before the sun was out.

He walked to his house with the McDonald's bag in hand. The $300 cash in his back pocket from his night's work made it all worth it. He saw his dad's car parked in their driveway.

Jimmy opened the front door and walked inside, not too concerned about being quiet. He turned on the hallway light and almost dropped his food when he saw his dad sitting silently on the couch in the living room. There was a thick shot of whiskey poured in his glass. The TV was turned off, and it seemed like his dad had been staring at the living room wall.

Their eyes met, and Jimmy swallowed what saliva was remaining in his mouth. His dad looked exhausted. Jimmy knew he had probably just gotten in from his own night shift. His shoulders were hunched over, and his bloodshot eyes looked sunken and defeated. Not unlike the man in the suit he had met earlier at the Delta Rise.

His dad managed half a nod as he stared into the eyes of a son he hardly knew. They both were aware that there would be no conversation about why Jimmy was just getting in now. One of them was too weak and exhausted to converse, and the other wouldn't tell the truth, in any case.

As Jimmy walked upstairs to his room, he didn't know how he felt, whether the unease in his stomach was resentment, pity, or guilt. Suddenly, the cash in his back pocket didn't seem quite so satisfying.

As he walked past his parents' bedroom, towards his own, he could feel his mom taking a deep breath and exhaling, knowing that her son was finally home. Jimmy knew she couldn't sleep until he was home safely.

– 7 –

Jimmy sat in class on Monday morning, making no effort to keep his eyes open. He was proud of himself for even managing to make it to class after his late night.

"Jimmy!"

His eyes sprung open. He felt there might have been drool hanging from the side of his mouth. He paid no attention to it.

"Yes, Ms. Chohan," he said, not even trying to hide the fact that he was hardly awake. He even produced a half yawn afterwards, which made the kids in class laugh.

"Oh good, you're alive," she said sarcastically. "I thought maybe my lecture had bored you to death."

"No way, ma'am. It was all very fascinating. So interesting, in fact, that I was closing my eyes so I could imagine what you were saying even better." The classroom snickered again.

"Ah well, I very much appreciate that. Please see me after class today. I would love to hear what your vivid imagination came up with from my lecture on pronouns and adverbs."

Jimmy nodded as he struggled to sit upright. He settled for having his elbow on the desk with his hand propping up his head.

After class, Jimmy sat watching his classmates scatter for lunchtime. Why couldn't he have had Math afterwards and not lunch? He had made plans with Gary and Mike to cruise down to McDonald's and munch some burgers.

When everyone had left, Ms. Chohan grabbed a chair and sat down across from Jimmy.

"So what's going on?" she asked.

"Uh, what do you mean, Ms. Chohan?" Jimmy tried to act dumb.

"Come on, Jimmy. You have five months left until you're done with high school for good. And then you don't have to look at this place ever again. The days when you do show up to class, your mind is somewhere else. And this past month, I don't know what's up with you. You haven't handed in one assignment, and you don't even try to hide it anymore. What's up?"

When Jimmy didn't respond, Ms. Chohan continued, seeming to choose her words very carefully.

"Five years ago, when you walked into this same classroom, you were a scrawny thirteen-year-old. You were intelligent, and you weren't afraid of speaking up. I would recite a piece of English literature and ask everyone what they thought the meaning of it was. You'd always have something intelligent to say. You were curious. You loved to read. And when you thought I was wrong, you would call me out. And when your classmates were having difficulties, you tried to help them. Do you remember that?"

Jimmy shrugged. "Kind of. Seems like a lifetime ago."

Those had been the days when Jimmy did give school every opportunity to offer him something of value. Because he knew he was good at it, and everyone told him how important an education was. So why not follow the crowd and see what he could learn? But the more he looked for the purpose of it all, the more he was of the opinion that there wasn't one.

"This may not be my place, but I saw who you were talking with at your last basketball game," Ms. Chohan said.

Jimmy felt his heart rate increase. He knew she was talking about Sunny—who was a Tamanawis alumni and a frequent spectator these days at Jimmy's basketball games. After their last game, Sunny had come down to the floor to congratulate him. Jimmy remembered seeing the unimpressed stares of the teachers.

"If you continue on in this way, you'll be going down a bad path. I hate to say it, Jimmy, but those guys are going in a direction you don't want any part of. Selling dope to kids or whoever else will buy it. That may seem cool now, but they're a cancer to our society."

He slowly stretched his neck from side to side as he contemplated how to respond.

"I really don't know what you want me to say, Ms. Chohan. I mean, I'm here. It isn't like I'm skipping out. And I am not trying to be rude, but what I do outside of school really isn't your business."

Ms. Chohan inhaled deeply before continuing.

"Do you ever even think about what you want in the long run or the direction you're going in? You've been around for what, seventeen years on this earth? I've been around a lot longer than you have. So I've seen things that you haven't. And those wannabe thugs couldn't make it in school, so now they resort to preying on the weak and the vulnerable."

"Wise words, ma'am. I'll make sure I note them down in my diary tonight."

Ms. Chohan shook her head. "You know you're failing right? And I was really hoping that you would listen to what I had to say. But if not, I have no choice but to speak with Coach Dhillon and Principal Nelson. I know basketball playoffs are coming up. But if you aren't passing your classes, I'm sure they'll both agree with me that there should be consequences."

Jimmy's heart began to race rapidly. If there was one thing that kept him coming to school, it was basketball. There were plenty of things he wanted to say to her, but he settled for an icy glare.

Karen was cute in an understated way. She was short and petit, and her hair was always parted neatly down the middle. She was Mike's girlfriend, and she and Jessica had become best friends since she had moved from Toronto nearly a year ago. They were on school council together.

"That sounds fun. I'm in," Jessica responded. "What do you think, Jimmy?"

Jimmy had a mouthful of Jessica's mom's lasagna as he shrugged his shoulders. "I have a family thing this weekend," he replied between bites. He already knew Sunny was going to ask him to work.

Karen looked from Jessica to Jimmy. She was sceptical of their relationship, and she wasn't shy about letting Jessica know, either. "You don't know Jimmy the way I know him. He has a totally different side to him. Just give him a chance," Jessica would tell her.

Jimmy scraped up the last few bites of Jessica's lunch before putting the fork back into her container.

"Give your mom my highest praise. That was delicious," Jimmy said, pushing the container back to Jessica.

"Haha, I will. She'll be thrilled," Jessica replied, putting the container back into her lunch bag.

"So what are you up to after school today?" Jessica continued to Jimmy.

Before he could respond, however, Mike and Gary came trudging up to the table. "What's upppp bitches," Mike said, plunking down a McDonald's bag on the table.

"Don't tell us we don't love you," Gary said to Jimmy, motioning to the bag.

"Couple of Big Macs. Have to get you fed and ready for playoffs. Where were you? We were looking for you."

Jimmy laughed. "I'm good. I just had a real meal thanks to Jess's mom." He pulled out one of the burgers and offered it to Jessica, who accepted it. She was still hungry, not having anticipated that Jimmy would eat her entire lunch.

"Thanks," she said to Jimmy.

"So you guys down for a double date this weekend?" Mike said to Jimmy and Jessica as he swooped down to kiss Karen. She allowed him a peck on the cheek. "You're coming, right?" Mike said to Jimmy. "I don't want to hear any of your bullshit about you having other things to do."

Jimmy's mind was elsewhere, still thinking about what Ms. Chohan had said. "I don't know, man. Probably not this weekend. I'll let you know," he replied indifferently.

Mike just shook his head. "The usual story. You guys hear about Arun Sandhu?" he asked, changing the subject. "He dropped 52 points on North Surrey last game."

Jimmy and Gary didn't offer much of a response other than a slight nod. Arun played for Tamanawis' rival school, Princess Margaret Secondary. Jimmy and Arun were widely regarded as two of the best players in the province. When they had played earlier in the season, Tamanawis had defeated PM with a last-second shot by Jimmy. After the buzzer had sounded, Arun and Gary had gotten into a scuffle that was broken up before it could escalate.

The lunch bell rang, signalling the start of the afternoon classes. Jimmy yawned loudly and had a strong wish to be in his bed. Realizing that he had Math and then Humanities only strengthened the urge to not be at school. But he knew that he couldn't skip too many more classes, so he struggled to his feet and headed to class.

− 9 −

IT WAS FRIDAY after school, and Jimmy walked into the changing room for basketball practice. It had been a tough few days since his forced sit-down with Ms. Chohan, and his mind had not stopped racing.

He hadn't told anyone what she had said, trying to pretend it hadn't happened. But anytime he would sit down to try to finish up an assignment, his mind would lead him in a different direction, and he would somehow end up smoking a joint. So when he entered the changing room and could hear his teammates joking and messing around, Jimmy felt tingles of irritation. His teammates had been very relaxed and laid back lately because of how they had been dominating other teams.

Jimmy saw that a group of his teammates were huddled around Mike, so he walked up to the group. "What's going on?" Jimmy asked.

His teammates turned around, and when they saw Jimmy, there was a collective grin. Mike was holding what seemed to be a newspaper article. When he saw Jimmy, he immediately swooped over and put his arm around his shoulders. "Oh shit... The all-star is here. We got a celebrity in our midst. Who's got the camera?" Mike shouted.

"What the hell are you going on about," Jimmy said as he ducked under Mike's grip and snatched the newspaper from him.

He saw a large image of himself that took up nearly half of the page. Underneath it ran the headline:

TAMANAWIS PHENOM HOPES TO LEAD TEAM TO FIRST PROVINCIAL APPEARANCE

Jimmy escaped the congratulations from his teammates and sat down, reading the article.

> Jimmy Bains piled in 34 points to lead his team past the tough Enver Creek Cougars and secure a division title for the Tamanawis Wildcats. The previously unknown Wildcats, who were an afterthought before the start of the season, have emerged as a tough-nosed, gritty team that resembles the play of their captain, Jimmy Bains.
>
> Jimmy is known to strike fear in the hearts of his opponents, with his unrelenting and warrior-like mentality. The six-foot-one guard is proficient from beyond the three-point line, but where he causes havoc for the opposing team is inside the paint. His speed and quickness allow him to penetrate past defenders with ease, and his strength and ferocity make him a handful for any forward to handle.
>
> Jimmy leads the league in scoring, averaging just a notch over 30 points per game. The one area of his game that may be questioned is his playmaking ability, as he is just averaging four assists. Nonetheless, he has his team primed to make their first-ever appearance in this year's provincials. It's no surprise that Jimmy has college coaches salivating at the prospect of coaching him next year.

After he had finished reading the article, Jimmy sat there, continuing to stare at his face in the picture. He wasn't entirely sure how he felt. He knew that he should have been elated about getting this well-deserved recognition. He knew he was one of the top players in the province. But that wasn't why he played. He played because he loved the game. Basketball was his salvation. It was his oasis from the trials and tribulations of life. And the part about college coaches salivating... He didn't know why, but it made him feel sick.

By this time, his teammates had left for the gymnasium, and he was alone in the changing room, still clutching the newspaper in his hand. It was crumpled from how firmly he was grasping it. He put it down and was prepared to head out to basketball practice when he looked at the headline story on the front page:

DRUGS, GUNS AND GANGS. WHY THE EAST INDIAN COMMUNITY IS REELING FROM YET ANOTHER SURREY SHOOTING, AND WHAT YOU CAN DO ABOUT IT

Jimmy wanted to laugh. *Another cracker pretending to know what's going on?* Beside the door to the gym was a trashcan. Jimmy walked over, crushing the newspaper into a small ball and tossing it in the garbage before joining his team for practice.

It began with their usual starting five doing a shell drill, where the focus was ball movement, and making the right pass, and guys being in the right position.

The relaxed and nonchalant attitude of the team had carried through from the changing room to practice. It seemed to Jimmy that they were simply going through the motions; there was no intensity to any of their movements.

So when Paul threw a lazy pass to Jimmy that was intercepted, Jimmy got right in his face. "What the fuck was that?" Jimmy yelled at Paul, who stared back at him for a moment before looking away. Jimmy then turned to the rest of the team. "What the fuck is going on, boys? Y'all think we're hot shit because we won a few games. If we're not getting better every practice, what the hell are we even doing here?"

Jimmy was hot, suddenly frustrated with his entire team and needing more from them. Coach Dhillon stood silently on the side, watching the situation transpire. He knew the other players respected Jimmy and his desire to win. Coach Dhillon definitely respected it. Jimmy had heart, no one could doubt that. But sometimes, his intensity could get the best of him.

Coach Dhillon was fairly tall and showed the remnants of having once been fit and muscular. He had a broad, burly frame but now packed a lot of his extra weight in his mid-section, and he was constantly complaining about his back. He had thinning grey hair and a grey goatee. In general, he had a laid-back attitude and expressed genuine compassion for his students and players.

Once Jimmy had finished his tirade, Coach Dhillon called the team in for a huddle. "I don't know what more is to be said. I would have tried to phrase it more eloquently, but hopefully the point has gotten across. We all know what our end goal is this year, and that's the Provincial Championship. We're not going to get there with practices like these. And if someone is hard on you, it's because he expects more out of you. We all need to be accountable to our teammates and ourselves. On and off the court." Coach Dhillon's eyes shifted to Jimmy when he said this. In that moment, Jimmy knew Ms. Chohan had talked to him.

"Okay, boys. Let's finish today's practice off with a scrimmage. Game-like mentality. Let's go. Shirts and skins."

Paul and Jimmy were on opposing teams, and they were defending each other. The intensity of Jimmy's message seemed to have trickled down to the rest of the team, and no one seemed more affected by it than Paul. Jimmy had never been defended like he was in that scrimmage. Paul was so close that Jimmy was sure Paul could smell the lunch on his breath. It was as if he was paying Jimmy back for cursing him out. Nonetheless, Jimmy loved the response and he loved the battle. It was as if he was sweating out all of his negative energy.

By the end of the scrimmage, Jimmy's team was down by one, and Jimmy was dribbling the ball near the top of the three-point line. Gary trudged up from the bottom of the key to set a pick on Paul. Jimmy used the screen to get free and penetrated hard to the hoop, with no defenders guarding the rim. Jimmy rose up for an easy lay-up, but Paul had shaken free of the pick and out of nowhere, lunged forward to block Jimmy's shot. Paul succeeded, but his momentum carried him into Jimmy, creating a ton of contact that would have meant a sure foul if it had been an actual game.

"Foul," Jimmy yelled as they both crashed to the floor.

Paul sprung to his feet and was screaming, "That ain't no fuckin' foul! That was all ball! Don't call that shit! Clean! ALL DAY, BABY!"

Jimmy was still lying on the floor, staring up at Paul. He had never seen the guy like this before. The rest of the team was looking on in disbelief too. Paul was usually quiet and reserved.

Jimmy slowly got to his feet as his team was busy arguing with Paul about the foul call. "That was clean," Jimmy said loudly. "All ball. You guys win."

Everyone on that floor knew it had been a foul.

Jimmy then turned to Paul. "That's what I need from you. Every goddamn time you're on this floor, that is what I goddamn need from you. Foul or no foul, you won your team that game."

The rest of the team went quiet as Paul looked at Jimmy, then simply nodded.

Coach Dhillon stood on the sideline, once again just observing, and now smiling to himself. Jimmy could do his job better than he could.

After they had all showered and changed, they were hanging out in the gym, talking about the upcoming weekend.

"Pauly boy, no studying this weekend. Put the books away for once, and we'll show you a good time, aight?" Mike said, throwing a playful jab at Paul.

"We'll see," laughed Paul. "Might have a family thing though."

Paul was the kind of kid you wanted your daughter to date. He was clean-cut, smart, and had self-control when it came to partying with kids like Mike, Jimmy, and Gary. He was also the second leading scorer on the basketball team, behind Jimmy. He was president of the school council and a shoo-in to be the class valedictorian, with all of his extracurricular activities and an impressive GPA.

Jimmy had never gotten on great with Paul. It wasn't just because he used to date Jess. They simply had nothing in common. Paul was a bookworm and Jimmy wasn't. All Jimmy really cared about was how Paul performed on the basketball court.

"Come on, buddy," Mike prodded Paul. "How can you be a part of the team if you're not down to chill ever with the boys?"

Paul laughed again. "We're chillin' right now."

"It's different, brah. I want to see that nasty streak some more like we saw today," Mike insisted.

"Aren't you supposed to go to the movies with your girl this weekend?" Jimmy interrupted.

Mike looked somewhat confused, then seemed to remember

his prior obligation with Karen. "Oh yeah, sorry boys, I'm out too. I'd rather chill with my girl than a bunch of dickheads like you anyways." Laughing, he turned to Jimmy. "What are you doing, anyways?"

"I'm busy."

"Sunny's got you grindin', eh." It was a statement rather than a question.

Jimmy didn't respond. He was hoping that word wasn't spreading about what he was up to with Sunny. The only person he had told was Gary.

As they were leaving, Coach Dhillon poked his head through the P.E. teacher's lounge, which led into the gymnasium.

"Jimmy, can I speak to you for a moment?"

"No problem, coach. I'll catch you guys later," Jimmy said to his teammates.

Jimmy took a seat in the lounge, across from Coach Dhillon. "Do you know why I asked to speak with you," his coach asked.

"To be honest, I was hoping that it would be about today's practice and how it seems like we're finally turning the corner. But I don't think that's what you called me in to talk about."

Coach Dhillon offered Jimmy half a smile. "How long have I been coaching you now, Jimmy?"

"Since grade eight, sir."

"And how would you say our relationship is?"

"It's been really good. You've always treated me well. And I've appreciated it."

Coach Dhillon took a deep breath as if he was preparing to say something that had been on his mind for a while. "I still remember the first time we met. It was at basketball tryouts in grade eight. Do you remember that?"

This was the second time this week a teacher was trying to

get him to remember back to his grade-eight self. Jimmy nodded, seeing where Coach Dhillon was trying to go with this.

"Between you and me, I didn't think this team was going anywhere. You all weren't that disciplined, and to be honest, you guys weren't that good. But you stood out. And it wasn't your talent. It was your love of the game. And look at you now. There isn't a player in this province that I would take over you. You have something that those other kids don't have. You have a sense of urgency now that I've never seen in you before. Like you're trying to cherish every moment you're on this court."

"Well, this is the last opportunity we have to make provincials, sir. I want to make the most of it," Jimmy replied.

"I understand that," Coach Dhillon continued. "And I'm really glad that's how you're approaching it. But I think it's something else. I think it's because once you finish school this year, you think that's it. You're approaching this as your swan song year, and you're going to hang 'em up after this."

"Well, it very well might be my last year playing basketball, sir."

"But why?" Coach Dhillon asked, getting visibly agitated. "You got more than enough talent to play at the next level. And it isn't just your talent and physical abilities. It's the way your team responds to you. They would run through a brick wall for you. You bring the most out of them. Why can't you see these qualities in yourself?"

Jimmy didn't know how to respond to this, so he stayed quiet and began looking at the floor, down towards his shoes.

"Jimmy, look at me," Coach Dhillon said quietly. When Jimmy looked up, Coach Dhillon was holding a handful of white envelopes in his hand. "Do you know what these are?"

"No, sir. What are they?"

"These are letters from different college coaches, expressing interest in you. I haven't responded to a single one, and you know why?" Jimmy shook his head. "Each one asks for your school transcript. And if I sent it to them, that would be it. They don't want a kid who can't even pass English. Ms. Chohan told me about what's going on in her class. I don't think you'll be surprised, but this isn't the first time that one of your teachers has approached me, concerned about you and your grades. Do you know what I tell them?"

Jimmy shook his head again, wanting nothing more than to not be there. "I tell them that basketball is what keeps you coming to school. Without basketball, who knows where you would be. And those older guys that you're hanging out with... You know you're so much better than that." Jimmy remained silent. "I know you got places to be, and I know you don't want to be here talking to me, so I'll get to the point," Coach Dhillon continued. "Ms. Chohan didn't just tell *me* about your troubles in class. She brought the principal into the meeting as well. And I don't have much sway over the principal. They simply asked me to deliver their message. If you want to continue playing basketball, there are two conditions. The first is that you must catch up on all of your school assignments. You must attend class on time, and be awake and alert, and be willing to participate."

Coach Dhillon paused as he waited for Jimmy's response. Jimmy nodded his acknowledgement of the condition. "And the second?"

"The second was Ms. Chohan's idea. We have arranged an appointment with the school counsellor, Mr. Pratt, for the end of next week. Maybe he can help you formulate some sort of plan for when you're done high school. Whatever that is, it's strictly between you and him. He's a good man."

Jimmy couldn't think of anything worse than to be cooped up with a dropout psychiatrist-turned-school-counsellor who wanted Jimmy to tell him about his feelings. "And if I don't?"

It was Coach Dhillon's turn to break eye contact. "Unfortunately, you'll be off the basketball team."

Jimmy stood up. Suddenly, he couldn't tolerate being here a second longer. And he did have places to be. "Is there anything else you need to talk to me about, sir?" he asked impatiently.

The pain in Coach Dhillon's eyes was obvious. He only wanted what was best for Jimmy. "That's everything."

Jimmy stomped out to his car and slammed the door shut, shaking his head in disgust at the thought of being forced to go to some washed-down version of therapy.

Why the hell do they even care about what I do, anyways? It's my life, and I should live it how I please. All these goddamn teachers act like they have it all figured out, like they have the wisdom. Like they know something I don't. They only know what they've been taught to teach. Nothing more. This is how people get sucked into the rat race. They fold. But not me. I ain't no chump. Screw 'em.

He pulled out his phone and saw he had two missed calls. One was from Sunny, the other from Jessica. He stared at the phone for a few moments before returning Sunny's call.

"Whatup, youngin," Jimmy heard Sunny's raspy voice say from the other end of the phone. He must have been smoking a joint.

"Chillin', just finished up ball practice. Whatup with you?"

"You gonna be the next Lebron or what. Saw your article in the paper. Props, little bro."

"Yeah, it's nothin'. They cover most teams in the province," Jimmy replied, trying to sound casual.

"Yeah, yeah." Jimmy could hear Sunny taking a drag. "Imma need you to work for me for a couple hours."

"When? Right now?" Jimmy asked, looking at the clock in his car. It was a quarter to five by this point.

"Yeah. Stop by right now. I'll have the stuff ready."

"Aight, I'll be there in ten."

– 10 –

As Jimmy had expected, Sunny asked him to work over the weekend as well. Sunny was beginning to rely on him much more than Jimmy had initially anticipated.

There was a strange allure to the drug game, Jimmy realized. It was like the streets were a drug of their own, and each time he was hustling, it was like taking another hit. The money was nice, but that wasn't the only thing that got him hooked. It was the adrenaline rush that he felt every time he had to go see someone. It was the laser-like focus he had to develop to sense when trouble was around. Jimmy finally felt like he was doing something with a purpose. He was on his grind. He was giving the people something that they wanted. No, something that they needed.

He was just finishing up his shift on Saturday night and was heading back to Sunny's house to return the product and the phone. It was nearing 2 a.m., and Sunny's cul-de-sac was deathly silent. The construction of the neighbouring houses was slowly progressing, but lumber and other material still littered the ground. Jimmy slowly made his way around the side of the house to Sunny's basement.

As he approached, he could hear a heated discussion coming from inside.

"I told you once. We ain't doing it. Not right now." Sunny's voice was aggressive, with hints of irritation.

Jimmy knocked on the door. The voices immediately stopped. "Who is it?" Sunny said. This time, his voice was quiet and nervous. The door swung open, and Jimmy was met with the heaving sounds of Ajay's breathing. The music was turned off, but the basement reeked of weed smoke.

Jimmy walked past Ajay without giving him a glance. Sunny gave Jimmy a slight nod and began pacing the room. There was a blunt hanging from the side of his mouth. "What's going on?" Jimmy asked.

Sunny stopped pacing mid-step and reached up to his mouth to find the blunt. He lit it, then took the first hit as if he was gasping for breath. He breathed in deeply, holding the weed smoke in his lungs much longer than usual. Jimmy had never seen Sunny so stressed. "Nothing," he finally answered.

Jimmy placed the line phone and the remaining product on the kitchen table. He had to push away a few empty McDonald's bags to find room. "Alright, then. Imma take off."

As Jimmy was headed to the door, Sunny called him back. "Have a drink with us." Jimmy had noticed a half-full vodka bottle on the living room table. Before he had a chance to respond, Sunny grabbed a glass and poured him a thick shot. He handed it to Jimmy, then refilled his own glass. "Cheers."

"Cheers." Jimmy drank it in one gulp.

Sunny passed him the blunt, and Jimmy took a drag. And then another. He passed it to Ajay. The big guy was antsy. His foot was fidgeting against the floor, and his eyes were darting back and forth. He looked very uncomfortable, as if he wanted to be doing something else.

Sunny poured up more shots. "Have a seat, lil man. Relax."

It took about an hour and a few more drinks before Sunny had finally evened out a bit. At that point, he revealed what had him so stressed out. "Some shit's going down right now. With the line."

"What you mean?" Jimmy asked.

"The guys we bought the line from had their own supplier. But I got my own connects, and I found someone that charges way less. But the dudes that were supplying the line before don't like that loss of business. So they've been on my case."

"So what does that mean?"

"It means they're trying to punk us," Ajay interrupted. "They think we're pussies and we'll pay the premium no questions asked. But that's money out of our pocket. Fuck that."

Sunny sighed as he lit up another joint. "Problem is, these guys are pretty big in the game. And they got a lot of muscle behind them. I'm just trying to figure this shit out."

"Ain't nothing to figure out," Ajay said. "We gotta build our own rep in the streets. We gotta tell 'em what's up."

Jimmy looked at Sunny and knew that he was torn. "So what you gonna do?"

Sunny took another deep draw of the joint before answering. "I don't know. Not yet."

Jimmy had nothing to say, and he accepted the joint when Sunny offered it to him. The energy in the room was tense, and Sunny continued to pace back and forth. Suddenly, he stopped as if he'd had some sort of epiphany.

"Fuck it. I ain't gonna let these bitches mess up my vibe. Trap party this Saturday. Imma invite all the chicks in my phone. We gonna get lit and rip shit up. You down?" He looked hard at Jimmy.

"Yeah, you know I'm always game."

- 11 -

THEY HAD THEIR final regular-season game on Tuesday against Guildford Park Secondary, and it was an absolute demolishment. Tamanawis won by twenty-eight points, and because of the win, they were guaranteed a bye in the first round of the playoffs. Jimmy piled in forty-one points and held the opposing team's best player to only two baskets. After the game, Coach Dhillon pulled Jimmy to the side and reminded him of his meeting with Mr. Pratt, which had been set for Thursday.

The nagging tension that had built up in his neck and his head continued to get worse, and at times it was unbearable. His head felt heavy, like the multitude of thoughts circulating through his mind were adding additional weight. He knew that Jessica could sense something was wrong. She had that ability. She also knew that the harder she pushed, the further Jimmy would distance himself.

It was Thursday at lunchtime, and Jimmy was sitting in the cafeteria. "What are you doing this Saturday?" Jessica asked. "Let's hang out."

Jimmy hadn't told her that he was going to Sunny's party. "Shit, I can't do that night. Maybe Sunday?" Jessica looked away. "What?" She brought her gaze back to Jimmy, and he could see that she was hurt but didn't want to admit it. "What?" Jimmy prodded again.

Jessica took a deep breath. "You know I don't ask for much. I do my own thing, and I let you do yours. But you're my boyfriend. I wish you would remember that sometimes."

Jimmy began to feel lightheaded and off balance. He felt stirrings of nausea, and suddenly the lights from the ceiling seemed oddly bright and distracting. He reached over and put his hand on top of hers. "I know. I'm sorry. Sunday, let's do something. I'm free the whole day."

"I'm not stupid. I know what you've been doing."

Jimmy glared at her for a few moments, not sure how to respond. "What do you mean?" he finally said.

"People talk, Jimmy."

Jimmy went quiet for a moment. "Paul getting into your ear? You know he's still into you, right?"

"People have seen you driving around and making drops," Jessica blurted out. "It's not just one or two people that have told me." It was obvious that this had been weighing on her for a while now. Then she looked directly into Jimmy's eyes. The softness of her gaze made him look away. "I want to be here for you," she said quietly. "You don't have to do what you've been doing, and always act like you're in control. You can be vulnerable with me."

Jimmy could feel his heart begin to race as he searched for a way out of the conversation. Her eye contact didn't waver as she continued to look at Jimmy, hoping he would finally open up to her.

"Look, Jess, I appreciate what you're saying. But I promise you that you have nothing to worry about. I'm good."

Jessica closed her eyes for a few moments, and when she opened them, the softness had been replaced by sadness. "I don't know if I can do this anymore," she said. "If you can't trust me and if you can't talk to me, then what are we even doing?"

Jimmy felt his shoulders tighten even more, and a dull sensation appeared in the pit of his stomach. And then suddenly, he felt angry. He stood up and he pushed his chair to the ground. A few juniors who were sitting at the next table looked over at the sound of the commotion. He put his hands on the table, and leaned forward, and spoke quietly so only she could hear. "You could never understand. You go home every day to your nice house and your perfect family. I live in a house that my parents can barely even afford to keep. Every day, I see my dad drinking away his misery at this fucked up life we got. If I want something, it's on me to get it. I don't rely on anyone."

Jimmy saw tears forming in the corners of Jessica's eyes, but he stormed away before he could see them fall.

Heading directly to his car, he drove to the place that always seemed to be able to calm him down. Once he'd reached the cage, he sat in his car for a few minutes, lost in thought.

I'm not going back to wearing taped up shoes and not having enough money to even buy a Big Mac. How can she expect me to choose between her and my money? She doesn't understand where I come from. She only knows one thing, and that's comfort. Not me. I'm comfortable being uncomfortable. I grind. I get money. This is what I'm good at. And what's the alternative? Be more like Paul? Fuck that guy. Fuck all of 'em.

Jimmy opened up his glove department. He always kept a spare joint for situations like this. Then he popped the trunk, stepped out of his car, and grabbed the basketball that was always there.

Before he had a chance to light the joint, he saw a figure walking through the parking lot towards the cage. Gary fumbled with the latch on the cage door before finally unlocking it and stepped inside.

"Jessica tell you I would be here?"

"You know she really cares about you, man."

Jimmy didn't respond as he pulled out a lighter and sparked

the joint. After taking a few deep puffs, he held the smoke in his lungs before finally exhaling. He instantly felt the effects of the THC enter his bloodstream, the familiar haze that followed, the calm.

He passed the joint to Gary, who accepted it and took a puff.

Jimmy suddenly felt the urge to confide in Gary. "Coach Dhillon called me into his office couple practices ago. He said if I don't pick up my schoolwork, then I'm done on the basketball team."

Gary's mouth dropped. "What? Dude, what the hell are you doing here then? You can't be skipping classes and getting high. What class you got next, anyways?" Jimmy had English with Ms. Chohan, and it wouldn't be long before class started and she noticed his empty seat. When Jimmy didn't respond, Gary continued. "We need you on the team, man. You need to be on the team. What else Coach Dhillon tell you?"

"They want me to meet with the school counsellor. Think his name is Mr. Pratt or something. So stupid."

"When is the meeting?"

"Today, after school." Just thinking about the meeting made Jimmy's mind begin to spin. He took another deep drag.

Gary walked right up to Jimmy, who noticed his pained expression. "You're like a big brother to me," Gary said in a voice barely above a whisper. "I care about you, bro. We all do. Without basketball, what the hell are you gonna do? Go to the meeting, bro. If you ain't gonna do it for you, do it for me."

- 12 -

It was 3 p.m., and Jimmy was standing outside Mr. Pratt's office. It had been a few hours since the joint at the cage, but he knew the high was still lingering. He hadn't gone to his afternoon classes, telling himself he needed the time to relax and unwind after what had transpired with Jessica.

He had popped a couple of drops of Visine into each eye and sprayed Axe on his clothes, to mask the smell of the weed. Jimmy knocked on Mr. Pratt's office door and held onto a glimmer of hope that there would be no response.

"Come in," a voice said from inside the office.

Jimmy sighed as he opened the door. He was surprised at the space, about half the size of a normal classroom, and much larger than Jimmy had expected.

There were two desks in the middle of the room, and a small leather couch pushed up against the wall opposite the door. At the back of the classroom was a massive bookshelf that must have been six feet high. It occupied the majority of the wall space and was totally full of books. On top of the bookshelf were a few framed pictures.

On what looked to be like an extremely comfortable and expensive black reclining chair, Mr. Pratt sat behind a beautifully crafted desk that had about half a dozen books scattered over it. He had been the school counsellor at Tamanawis since the day the school had opened over two decades earlier.

"Hello," he said. "Jimmy, I presume?" He stood up and walked around his desk to greet Jimmy. When Jimmy shook his hand, he realized how gigantic Mr. Pratt's was. It enveloped Jimmy's and imparted a grip that left his hand feeling a little sore.

The counsellor was much taller than Jimmy had expected. He looked to be in his early sixties and had a lean but athletic build, short white hair, and a trimmed white beard below sharp, pronounced facial features. But what Jimmy noticed most were his eyes—bright blue but with hints of green, quiet yet attentive, gentle yet penetrating.

"It's very nice to meet you," Mr. Pratt said politely.

Jimmy nodded but didn't say anything in return. He took his backpack off his shoulder and sat in one of the two chairs opposite the large desk.

Mr. Pratt did not return to his chair, instead sitting on the edge of his desk, looking at Jimmy, who felt exposed. It was almost as if the man could see past his façade and into his depths.

"So what brings you in today, Jimmy?" he asked.

"It wasn't my decision. I don't want to be here," Jimmy blurted out.

Mr. Pratt smiled gently. "I understand that, Jimmy. Let me rephrase it. What circumstances led to you being obliged to be here?"

Jimmy hesitated, wondering how many details he wanted to fess up to. "Just haven't been doing as well in school as some of my teachers want. So they're making me catch up on some of my schoolwork. If I don't, they're saying I'm off the ball team."

Mr. Pratt tilted his head to one side, as if a little confused. "Well then why do they have you coming to see *me*? There are quite a few school-appointed tutors who could assist you with your schoolwork much more than I can."

Jimmy shrugged. "Honestly, I have no idea. I just want to get this over with."

The counsellor then gave Jimmy a curious look. His eyes fixed on Jimmy's, and he squinted slightly as if trying to see something. His lips curled into a small smile. "You're high," he said.

"What?" Jimmy exclaimed, suddenly becoming very defensive. "No I'm not."

Mr. Pratt didn't immediately respond. Instead, he looked out a window that had a nice view of a cluster of trees situated at the back of Tamanawis. His gaze returned to Jimmy. "What's going on, Jimmy?"

Jimmy could feel his heart rate begin to increase, as thoughts began to swirl through his mind. "Nothing. Just want to get this over with."

"You're lost, aren't you?" Mr. Pratt said in a voice so gentle that it sent shivers up Jimmy's spine. The words seemed to paralyze Jimmy, who simply stared at Mr. Pratt for a few moments. And then he felt his blood begin to boil, his body becoming very hot.

"What the fuck do you know?" he retorted standing up. "I'm not the one who's been cooped up in this shitty office for the past twenty years and doesn't wanna retire because you're either too broke or ain't got shit all to do."

Mr. Pratt didn't react in the slightest, but just continued to sit on the edge of his desk and surveyed Jimmy in a way that made the boy's skin tingle.

"I wish you the best, Jimmy," he said finally. "I can't help people who aren't ready to be helped. You can see yourself out." With that, he walked back around his desk and sat down in his reclining chair, then picked up the book that he had previously laid down on his desk and flipped to the page that he had bookmarked.

Jimmy stood there, and Mr. Pratt's peaceful demeanour only angered him more. "Fuck you. You ain't know shit." With that, Jimmy stormed out, slamming the door behind him.

- 13 -

It was Saturday evening, and Jimmy was getting dressed for Sunny's party. Jimmy's bedroom door was cracked open, and he could hear his dad and Inder laughing and joking downstairs.

Inder was Jimmy's dad's oldest friend from when they lived in India. Inder was in Surrey for a few weeks, visiting some friends and family. Sometimes Jimmy would hear his dad talking on the phone with Inder in the early hours of the morning. There would usually be a glass of whiskey in front of him as they reminisced about childhood.

After picking out his freshest pair of Jordan's, Jimmy admired himself in his closet mirror, then looked at his watch and saw that he still had some time to kill; it was only 9 p.m., and he didn't want to show up to Sunny's until the party was already in full gear.

Jimmy heard someone knock lightly on his door. "Come in."

His mom peeked her head through. "Hi, sweetie, where are you off to tonight?"

"Just headed to a party soon. Gonna leave in a little bit here."

"Oh, okay. Well, if you have time before you need to go, I'm sure your dad and Inder would love for you to say hi."

Jimmy shrugged. "Yeah, maybe I'll come down for a few minutes."

"Okay, I will let them know." Jimmy's mom smiled as she closed the door quietly behind her.

After checking himself out in the mirror for a few more minutes and making sure that his outfit couldn't be more perfect, Jimmy headed downstairs and into the living room.

"Jimmy! Come have a drink with us," his dad yelled over. It was obvious he'd already had a few stiff ones.

"What you guys drinking?" Jimmy replied, just out of habit. Jimmy's dad and all of his older relatives only drank one thing: Crown Royal.

Jimmy's preference was vodka. When Jimmy was in grade eleven, he, Mike, and Gary would stand outside the liquor store, asking brown guys his dad's age to buy them a bottle of Smirnoff. Those men were usually the most accommodating. The boys would pass the guy an extra ten dollars for his trouble. Then they would typically head to the cage, usually drinking straight out of the bottle, with a two-litre of 7-Up on the side to mask the taste. Sometimes, if they were lucky enough, Mike's parents would be out, and Mike would invite them over to his dad's man cave in the basement.

"I guess I don't have any other options," Jimmy laughed when he saw only the Crown Royal. He grabbed himself an empty glass and poured a thick drink.

The older men were sipping their Crown straight. Jimmy's dad had the weekend off, a rare event, which meant that the sixty-ounce bottle sitting on their living room table might not even last them until tomorrow.

Jimmy shook his head as he poured a generous amount of Coke that he got from the fridge to mix with the Crown.

"How do you guys drink that straight?" Jimmy asked them. "It's so bitter."

The two friends laughed together. "You'll see when you get older," Jimmy's dad said. "You might not drink it now, but just wait. One day, you'll realize that whiskey is in our blood. Born from the Punjab, we were born to drink whiskey and nothing else."

Jimmy shook his head again as he took a sip of his drink, which actually wasn't bad.

"So how's basketball?" Inder asked Jimmy.

"It's good. Playoffs start soon. You guys should come down and watch a game."

Jimmy's dad smiled proudly. "For sure, son. We will come and cheer you on."

Inder nudged Jimmy's dad. "Maybe sneak a few pegs of Crown in our cups." They laughed again. "Has your dad ever told you about what a star he was at cricket back in India?"

Jimmy shook his head. In all his years growing up, his dad had never mentioned anything about cricket. Jimmy had always figured that his dad's best and only skill was how much alcohol he could consume.

His dad tried to wave Inder off, but Inder continued. "Your dad was the best player in our village. Up until he met your mom, it was almost a certainty that he was going to play professional."

"What?" Jimmy exclaimed, turning to his dad. "How come you never told me?"

"It's nothing," his dad answered, taking a big gulp from his drink.

"What happened?" Jimmy asked Inder.

"Well, they had the opportunity to move to Canada. And I guess your dad thought that in the long run, raising a family in Canada would make more sense. I can't believe you didn't know."

"No, I didn't," Jimmy said, leaning back into his seat and feeling a pang in his stomach. He had sometimes wondered where he got his athletic abilities.

While Jimmy was lost in thought, his dad had poured three more hefty shots of Crown. He gave one to Jimmy and one to Inder. Jimmy raised his glass and said, "Cheers. To my dad."

"Cheers," they both said.

Jimmy could have sworn that he saw a tear glistening in the corner of his dad's eye.

"So what else have you been up to?" Inder asked Jimmy. "I'm sure there is only so much basketball you can play."

Jimmy hesitated as he looked at Inder, who was staring at him curiously. "You know, just things high school boys do, I guess," answered Jimmy.

"Not getting into too much trouble?" continued Inder, who seemed to have an agenda with his questions.

Jimmy shook his head. "I'm sure not much more trouble than you and my dad got into when you were younger."

Jimmy's dad laughed as Inder's mouth curled into a sly smile. "Well, we came from a different time and a different place," Inder responded. "We didn't have the luxuries you have. We would have killed to be in your position growing up. You should really appreciate how lucky you have it."

Jimmy glared at Inder. He didn't know why he was being interrogated in his own house, and he suddenly felt an urge to put Inder in his place and educate him about a few things. Before he could, Jimmy's dad interrupted, as if sensing the tension that had sprung into the air.

"Jimmy just had an article about him written in the newspaper. I think I already told you about it. But he is quite the athlete. They even talk about him playing in college," his dad said to Inder.

"Yeah, you told me about it," Inder replied but continued to stare at Jimmy. "So, you planning to go to college?"

"We'll see how things go," Jimmy answered rudely.

Jimmy's dad did the only logical thing that seemed to relieve the tension in the room: poured another shot for each of them.

An hour passed in less tricky conversation. The bottle of Crown had a sizeable dent in it, and they were all feeling the effects. Jimmy had a healthy buzz and told them that he had to get going. His dad excused himself to go to the washroom, saying goodbye to Jimmy.

"I still remember the last time I came to visit. You were just a little boy," Inder told Jimmy as he put on his jacket. "Your dad would hold you in his arms, and you would have your little hands wrapped around his finger. He would refuse to put you down."

Jimmy could feel his neck begin to stiffen up. He offered Inder half a smile as he grabbed his car keys and turned towards the door.

"Jimmy," Inder said, his voice becoming much lower. "Your dad and mom might not say anything to you, but they know. They know where you're going when you're out until morning, and how you can afford those new shoes and clothes. And new car." Inder motioned to the car keys. "Your dad mistakes his kindness for love. When you talk back to him and your mom, it breaks their heart. You are their biggest weakness."

"You don't know what you're talking about," Jimmy snorted back.

"And you do," Inder retorted with his eyes fixed on Jimmy. "You're just a kid. Maybe instead of causing all this grief to your parents, give them something to be proud of."

Jimmy stood there, halfway to the door, not even searching for words. He knew there were none. Without even a nod of acknowledgement, he took the final few steps to the door, walking out into the winter evening.

He sat in his car for a while, deep in contemplation. His mind drifted to his dad when he would have still been in India. It was difficult for Jimmy to imagine his dad as a sports star, or even as having a life before him.

No way dad could have played professional. I mean, look at him. He's no athlete. Inder was probably just exaggerating. Wouldn't be surprised. They moved to Canada so they could all have a better life. Not just me. They can't blame me for that.

"They never have blamed you. They've never blamed you for anything," another voice in his head answered.

Why didn't Dad ever tell me about his childhood or his talent at cricket?

"Have you ever shown any interest? In anything they do?"

So what? It's my fault that Dad didn't get to pursue his dreams? That he has to work two jobs just to pay the bills? Why he stays awake in the early morning, staring at the wall? It's not my fuckin' fault.

Jimmy could feel his heart beating more rapidly. There were small beads of sweat forming on his temple, and it felt like he had a brick in his stomach.

Jimmy knew he mistreated his parents and took advantage of their kindness, but he told himself it wasn't intentional. There had just never been any fear of consequences for his actions. He was doing what he was doing so he didn't have to rely on them or ask them for things that he knew they couldn't provide. In the end, he wanted to take care of his parents. He loved and appreciated his mom and dad. He was grinding now so he could reap the benefits later. For all of them.

As Jimmy pulled out from the side of the road, his neck and head continued to throb with discontent. He couldn't help but continue to feel the sting of Inder's words, like a wasp that refused to let go.

- 14 -

JIMMY HAD CONVINCED Gary to come with him to Sunny's party. He could tell Gary was hesitant about being around drug dealers and so many people older than him. But in the end, Jimmy had convinced Gary, like he knew he would.

They lived only a couple of blocks apart, so a few minutes later; Jimmy was parked in front of his house. Gary, his mom, and his younger sister lived in a two-bedroom basement suite. Gary's mom and sister shared one room, and Gary had the other. Jimmy had only been inside on a handful of occasions.

When he saw Gary approaching, Jimmy unlocked his car door. Gary was actually wearing jeans today and not his customary sweatpants.

"Whatup bro?"

"Ah shit," Jimmy replied. "Look at you all dressed up. And shee-it, is that cologne I can smell?"

"Ha, get out of here."

Jimmy just grinned as he pulled away from the curb.

It was just after 11 p.m. when Jimmy turned into Sunny's block. The sides of the road, usually empty, were now occupied with cars on both sides. As Jimmy drove by Sunny's house, looking for a parking spot, he could hear music coming through his half-opened window.

"Daymn, the party has started," Jimmy said. When he didn't hear a reply, he peeked over at Gary, who seemed to be sweating. "You aight, bro?" Jimmy asked.

"I'm just a little nervous man," Gary responded. "All these guys are older than us, and fuck, man… They might punk us."

Jimmy finally found a spot to park, and turned off the ignition. He turned to Gary, who looked as pale as Jimmy had ever seen him.

"Bro, you know who you rollin' with," he said to Gary. "I got respect from these guys, man. You ain't got nothin' to worry about. We'll get a couple of drinks in you, and you'll be flyin' high. Maybe even find you a female, ha."

Gary managed a laugh, and they both stepped out of the car. "Doesn't Sunny live in the basement? What landlord would let him throw a party?" Gary asked, looking curiously at Sunny's house. Jimmy had wondered the same thing, but Sunny had never brought it up.

On the side of the road, directly in front of Sunny's house, was a group of brown guys, huddled. They were shamelessly passing around a forty-ounce bottle of Crown, taking turns to swig from the bottle while using a two-litre of Coke to chase it down. It also looked like they had two or three joints circulating. Even from a distance, Jimmy could hear their conversation.

"And then buddy got in my face," one of them said loudly. "And so I fuckin' clocked buddy. Bitch was snoring on the sidewalk." The entire group laughed.

Jimmy didn't recognize any of the guys. When Jimmy and Gary got nearer to the house, the group stopped talking. Jimmy vaguely heard one of the guys whisper something. They all turned their heads and stared at Jimmy and Gary with an almost identical expression on their faces: their eyes narrowed, and they tilted their heads back a little as if they trying to seem taller and more intimidating. Two of the guys who were obviously steroid junkies pushed their chests out as far as they could, and Jimmy knew they were trying to flex their muscles to show how tough they were.

Jimmy found the scene almost comical. He had met too many of these types to think they were anything more than just punks. The kind of guys who were too afraid to talk to a girl, so they would just get hammered and search out a fight. Jimmy had to hold back his laughter, but he could sense Gary tense up beside him.

As they walked along the side of the house, Jimmy could see people scattered in the backyard as well. There was a distinct marijuana aroma coming from both directions. People were talking loudly, almost yelling because of the loud trap music playing from the basement's open door.

A couple of girls were standing just outside the basement door, holding red cups. One of them was a bigger girl wearing a short black skirt and lace-patterned panty hose. A revealing blouse showed off her massive breasts. Jimmy wondered what kind of bra she had to wear to push up breasts that probably otherwise sagged to the ground.

But her friend was cute and petit, and she was white, which was always a delicacy at parties like these. She was wearing jeans that complimented her butt very nicely, and simple black heels. She also had supple, perky tits, and Jimmy couldn't help but imagine how they would feel in his hands. Her makeup wasn't overdone—just a bit of eyeliner and mascara, and a simple lipstick—and she had light brown hair. Her smile was innocent and seductive, but her eyes cried out that she liked to live on the wild side. She looked a little younger as well, and Jimmy wouldn't have been surprised if they were the same age.

The bigger girl was talking animatedly to her cute friend and used her hands a lot when she spoke. When the cute friend saw Jimmy, she took a swig of her drink and eyed him curiously over the brim of the red cup. The bigger girl noticed that her friend had stopped paying attention and turned around to see what she was looking at.

"Whatup, girls," Jimmy said coolly.

The bigger girl's eyes darted from Jimmy to Gary. "Hi!"

Jimmy held out his hand, and the bigger girl shook it. "I'm Jimmy. And this is Gary," he said, making sure to ignore the pretty girl. He would pay her attention at some point, but this wasn't the time. "What you sippin'?"

"Vodka and seven," the bigger girl replied. "You wanna try some?" she said, holding out her drink.

"Nah, I'm gonna stick with Crown tonight. Imma go grab one. I'll holler at you guys in a bit. Didn't catch your name, by the way."

"I'm Alisha," she answered. "And this is my friend Jenny."

Jimmy gave Jenny a brief nod as he opened the door to the basement. Gary followed closely behind.

There were more people than Jimmy had expected, but the ratio of guys to girls at the party was at least two to one. There were guys leaning up against the wall talking to their friends but eyeing down the girls, taking big swigs of their drinks, trying to find the liquid confidence to talk to them. It kind of reminded Jimmy of an elementary school dance, when the boys and girls would stand on opposite sides of the gym. Except that now, there was alcohol involved, and all the guys seemed to have tattoos.

The round table usually in the middle of the kitchen was pushed up against the wall, so there was a large empty space in the middle in case people wanted to dance. There must have been two ounces of weed sitting on top of the table. Two guys were rolling up blunts, their eyelids drooping so low that Jimmy couldn't even tell whether they were open.

A half-dozen girls were sitting on the couches in front of the TV, and sixty-ounce bottles of Grey Goose and Crown Royal were perched in the middle of the coffee table. The girls had already put sizeable dents in both bottles. Their faces were caked with makeup, and they all kind of looked and dressed the same. They were making a feeble attempt at taking a selfie. Jimmy laughed when he saw them all trying to find their signature pose, pouting their lips and tilting their heads to show off their best side. Jimmy also observed a few couples leaning against each other and not making any effort to be social. It was like they were attached at the hip.

Jimmy recognized a handful of the guys in the basement but didn't see Sunny or Ajay. "Hey, you guys know where Sunny is?" he asked one of the guys rolling a blunt.

"Bedroom," he responded without even looking up.

Jimmy motioned to Gary to follow him, then knocked on the bedroom door. "Who is it?" a deep, gruff voice snarled—Ajay's.

"Jimmy."

Jimmy heard the door unlock, and he saw Sunny's grinning face. "Young buck," he bellowed, grabbing Jimmy by the shoulder and putting him in a friendly headlock that Jimmy did not appreciate.

"You know Gary, right?" he said to Sunny once he had escaped.

"Yeah, yeah, I know the big man. Whatup, G," Sunny said. They shook hands.

Jimmy looked over towards a desk in the corner of Sunny's room. Ajay was sitting on the desk chair with Harp, one of Ajay's good friends.

Harp was short and skinny with a bad complexion and wore a turban. Word on the streets was that he always kept a shank in his pocket and wasn't afraid to use it. Jimmy had always found the turban comical, since Harp must have disobeyed almost every rule that it represented.

Harp was using a debit card to chop up some white powder on the desk.

"You guys down to do a line?" Sunny asked them.

Jimmy shook his head. "Nah, I'm straight." Gary remained quiet as he eyed the white powder, so Jimmy spoke for him. "We're both straight. We can use a drink, though."

"Aight, aight, let's go get you one then."

They headed back out into the main area of the basement. By this point, Jenny and Alisha were back inside and sitting with the two guys rolling up the weed. Jimmy ignored them as he walked by but noticed Jenny looking at him.

"What you drinkin' then, foo," Sunny asked.

"Crown," Jimmy replied.

Sunny turned to Gary. "You don't talk much do you?"

"I'll have the same," stuttered Gary.

Sunny laughed. "Aight."

There were bottles of alcohol throughout the basement, but Sunny headed to the couch where the group of girls were still sitting and reached to grab the bottle of Crown Royal.

"Whatup, ladies. You don't mind, do you?" Sunny said, trying his best to be flirtatious. Jimmy snickered. The girls were preoccupied, with trying to take either the same selfie or a new one.

"Yo, big man, grab a couple cups," Sunny said to Gary, who nodded and headed to the counter, where there was a stack of them.

"You girls need a hand?" Jimmy asked as he observed the girls continuing to struggle with taking a picture they could post on their Instagram or Snapchat.

"Sure," one of them said as she passed Jimmy her phone.

It seemed like Jimmy had a natural talent for taking pictures, because all the girls agreed to use his picture to post.

"We haven't seen you at one of Sunny's party before. I'm Kim," said the girl who had handed Jimmy her phone. She had fake eyelashes that were as big as Jimmy had ever seen, and her hair was dyed a bright blonde. She was cute but definitely not Jimmy's type.

Before Jimmy could respond, Sunny had finished pouring his and Gary's drink, and Jimmy took a big swig. Sunny poured it really strong, and it tasted more bitter than what Jimmy was accustomed to.

Jimmy, Gary, and Sunny hung out with the group of girls for the next hour or so. They seemed to have taken a liking to Jimmy, and Sunny noticed. "Y'all might not know… But this is my prodigy," Sunny boasted to the girls as he put his arm around Jimmy's shoulders. "I've taught him 'bout the streets and 'bout the hustle. He's my lil bro."

"Oh, you're a dealer?" Kim asked.

Jimmy nodded and thought this would turn the girl off. But to the contrary, she batted her eyelashes a few times and toyed with her hair, and Jimmy was certain she was interested.

He was halfway through the second drink that Sunny had poured, and he was feeling really good. But it was different than an alcohol buzz. He turned to Sunny and leaned in to whisper, "You put anything in my drink?"

Sunny grinned slyly. "Don't worry about it, brah. Just a little molly. Ajay put it in all the two-litres of Coke and Seven-up. Everyone here is probably rollin'. Gotta make sure they have a good time. You know how it is."

Jimmy began to feel the first signs of tension pulsate in his shoulders. But his buzz was strong, so he just shook his head at Sunny and took another sip of his drink. The tension dissipated, and he leaned back into his chair. He couldn't deny that he was feeling good.

"Atta boy," Sunny said, slapping his back. "These girls are down, man. Already know you got Kim on lock. She can't stop looking at you. Screw it, tho. I'll take whatever is left, ha."

Jimmy turned around to say something to Gary, but he was nowhere in sight. He did see Jenny and Alisha, who were talking to the same group of guys he had seen outside. One of the guys was holding the same forty-ounce bottle of Crown Royal, but by this point, it was nearly empty. They were all extremely drunk, and Jimmy could hear from the couch their slurred words, which hardly sounded like English. It was obvious they were all trying to get Jenny's attention, but she seemed uninterested. Her gaze wandered off, and she caught Jimmy staring at her.

Jimmy didn't really care, and he held a steady gaze. She looked directly back at him, ignoring a guy who was offering her a shot.

Jimmy slammed back the rest of his drink as he turned to Sunny. "Who are those guys, anyways?" He motioned to the group surrounding Jenny.

Sunny craned his neck to look. "Those guys," Sunny said. "I graduated with them. All my age. They whatever."

"Any of them in the game?"

Sunny grinned. "Couple of 'em. But low-level shit. They all pretty much tried it but couldn't last. A few are trying to bust out a few courses at Kwantlen College now. Couple of them in real estate and whatever. But they don't do much. They turn up every couple days and smoke weed by the ounce. Come on, let me introduce you."

Jimmy had no real desire to meet them, but Sunny had stood Jimmy up and was leading him over. Kim and her friends were preoccupied with taking another selfie anyways.

"Whatup, Sunny," a couple of them said. Sunny had his arm around Jimmy's shoulders, and a couple of the guys glared at Jimmy suspiciously.

"Sup, boys," Sunny hollered. "Want to introduce you to my boy. A young OG in the making, and a basketball phenom. This is Jimmy." A couple of them simply nodded in Jimmy's direction, but most acted as if Jimmy wasn't there. He could feel Jenny's eyes glued on him. "Shit, and who this?" Sunny whistled, taking a step back as he admired Jenny.

She giggled. "Hi, I'm Jenny," she said to Sunny, holding out her hand.

"Shee-it, we don't do handshakes here," Sunny said as he took his arm off Jimmy. He gave Jenny a hug, pushing his body right up against hers, and Jimmy felt himself cringe slightly.

The group of guys seemed to have redirected their focus to Alisha, apparently accepting that Jenny was not interested but Alisha at least was willing to reciprocate their attention.

Jenny turned to Jimmy and smiled. Up close and in the bright lights of the basement, he noticed she had bright green eyes. "Hi, we met earlier, outside. You said you were gonna holler later, but you never did," Jenny said.

"Yeah, sorry. Bunch of people here that I hadn't met before, so I kinda had to make my rounds, I guess. How's your night going?"

"It's going okay, I guess. So how do you know Sunny?"

Before Jimmy could respond, Sunny had grabbed the bottle of Grey Goose from the table by the couches and was offering Jenny a shot.

Jimmy excused himself to go to the washroom. He was feeling on a different level as he stood in the washroom, leaning against his hands on the counter. He turned the knob to freezing cold water and washed his face, relishing how the water seemed to rinse away his impurities.

He was high.

He let the drips of water hang on his face and slowly trickle down into the sink. The liquor and the drugs had released him from the heaviness of all his problems. He didn't feel tense or anxious. He was in a fog of drunkenness, and he felt clear and relaxed.

He examined his face in the mirror. His eyes were hazy and droopy yet quiet and undisturbed. They stared intensely back at him. He moved his face closer to the mirror.

He heard the rhythmic beatings of his heart and felt vitality course through his body. In the background, he could hear the ramblings of his mind. His attention went there.

High as a motherfucker. This is what life's about. Why can't life always be this simple? This is why I get messed up. It's an escape from all the problems and the bullshit. This is the reason right now.

He heard the voice in his head like it was something apart from him.

He was drying his hands when he heard a knock on the washroom door. "Just one minute," he replied. But the knock came again, so he shook his head and opened the door. It was Jenny. She was holding her red cup in one hand as she stared up at him.

"Hi," she said softly.

"Hey, what's up? I'm done anyways. It's all yours."

Jimmy began to walk out the door, but Jenny moved slightly to block his path. Jimmy stopped, and she gently placed her hand on his chest and pushed him back into the washroom, then closed the door behind her.

"You know, I recognized you," she said. "From the newspaper article. You go to Tammy."

Jimmy nodded.

"I go to PM," she continued, putting her cup on the washroom counter.

"What you doing at this party then? Ain't you a bit young to be here?"

She smiled but didn't laugh as she began walking towards Jimmy. He felt himself taking a few steps back until he reached the corner of the washroom and couldn't retreat any further. Jenny continued to slowly advance, her eyes never leaving his.

"I could ask you the same thing," she said when she was only a foot away. Jimmy could smell the alcohol on her breath.

Jimmy didn't say anything. The silence hung in the air for a few moments. She took one more step in, and now Jimmy felt her body against his. He felt himself begin to get aroused, and he knew that she could feel it too. Without warning, his mind drifted off to Jessica.

He leaned back against the wall, trying to create a little distance between them. Jenny put her hand back onto his chest and this time, grasped his shirt. She pulled his head down as she stood up on her tiptoes. Their lips met in the middle, and her tongue instantly invaded his mouth. Jimmy's mind was still racing, and he made a half-hearted attempt to back away. But Jenny's hands reached around towards the back of his neck and pulled him in aggressively. This time, she went in full throttle, and it almost felt like she was trying to eat Jimmy's mouth.

Her hands retreated back down to Jimmy's chest and then lower, to his stomach, until her hands reached down and undid his belt. She began to massage him through his jeans. She stopped kissing Jimmy briefly as her attention turned towards his jeans buttons. He could hear her panting as she struggled to unbutton them. Once she finally did, she pulled down his pants and boxers in one go, then began to kiss Jimmy once more.

"Tell me what you want," she moaned through a kiss.

Jimmy's mouth went dry as he searched for a response. He noticed her cup still sitting on the counter. He reached forward and grabbed it. This time, he didn't care if there was ecstasy or whatever else in the drink. He just needed to be more messed up. He chugged it in one go.

"What, you nervous?" she joked playfully.

Jimmy managed a small laugh. "Nah, I'm chillin'."

She grinned as if she could sense his hesitation. Her lips left his and moved down to his neck. She continued to descend along his body, kissing his chest and then his stomach. By this point, Jimmy knew he couldn't stop her.

She gazed up at him with her light-green eyes. "You gonna fuck me now?"

Jimmy paused and then realized he hadn't come prepared that night. "Shit," he said to Jenny. "I ain't got no wrapper."

She shook her head. "It's all good."

Jimmy felt his heart begin to race, and he knew it was more than just the ecstasy.

As she pulled off her shirt and began to unbutton her own jeans, there was suddenly a loud crackling noise that sounded like firecrackers from somewhere outside.

"What the hell was that?!"

"Don't worry about it," Jenny replied. "It's probably nothing." But before she could even take off her jeans, there was another loud commotion and the sound of someone yelling.

"Yo, we gotta go check that out," Jimmy said as he pulled up his pants. He didn't wait for Jenny to respond as he opened the washroom door and walked out. As soon as he turned the corner into the living room, everyone seemed to be freaking out.

Jimmy saw Kim, and she seemed to be in tears. He approached her cautiously. "Hey, Kim, what just happened?"

"Those fucking bitches," she screamed.

"What?" Jimmy repeated and put his hand on her shoulder, trying to calm her down.

"What happened?" She attempted to gasp out a deep breath but was too overwhelmed with emotion and started sobbing again. Jimmy shook his head and looked for someone else to explain the situation.

The door to the basement swung open, and in walked Ajay, Sunny, and Harp. They seemed to be in a panic. Jimmy's heart dropped when he saw Gary walk in after them. They were in the middle of a heated discussion as they moved into a corner of the kitchen, away from everybody else.

Jimmy stormed up to Gary and swung him around. "Yo, Gary, what the fuck is going on?"

Gary's eyes were bloodshot, and he kept sniffing as if he had a runny nose. "Those muthafuckas," Gary slurred. "Those muthafuckas just shot up Sunny's house. We about to get those muthafuckas back."

Jimmy turned to Sunny. "Yo, Sunny man, what just happened? Your house just got shot up?"

Sunny's eyes were consumed with a fiery rage as he turned to Jimmy. "Yeah, those fuckin' pussies. They're dead. Nobody fucks with me. This is my hood. You down to roll?"

Jimmy could hear his heart beating through his shirt, but he took a deep breath, trying to get a handle on the situation. "You think that's a good idea, man? We're all messed up right now. And what if the cops show? Let's see what up tomorrow."

Sunny sneered at Jimmy. "I thought you were a rider. Guess not. Your fuckin' boy is down," he said, motioning towards Gary, who nodded animatedly.

"Yeah, I'm down. Let's get 'em, Sunny."

Jimmy knew that Gary had a lot more than just alcohol in his system. He should have never left Gary alone.

Ajay put his arm around Gary, embracing him. "You a real homie. Ya heard me? You roll with us and we gotch you," Ajay hollered.

"Yo, Ajay. He ain't rollin' with you guys," Jimmy said firmly.

Ajay took his arm off Gary's shoulders and turned towards Jimmy. His mouth curled into a smile. "What? You gonna stop me?" Ajay smirked. "How you gonna stop me? Show me."

Ajay stepped towards Jimmy until he was only a few inches away from his face. Jimmy felt unusually calm. "You a bitch," Ajay whispered to Jimmy. "I've been telling Sunny to drop your punk ass."

Jimmy didn't respond with any words. Instead, he simply glared into Ajay's eyes. He wasn't scared of him in the slightest. To Jimmy, Ajay's life was a failure. He was a drug addict, overweight, unsocial, and he compensated by trying to act like he was tougher than everybody else.

Ajay seemed unsettled that Jimmy wouldn't look away, as if he was looking right through him. He turned away from Jimmy and refocused his attention on Gary. "Gary, who you wanna roll with? Us or your bitch-ass friend?" Ajay snorted.

Suddenly, Gary looked flushed. Jimmy spoke before he had an opportunity to reply. "It ain't up to Gary. He ain't going."

Ajay wheeled around again to Jimmy, but this time anger was etched across the lines of his face. He shoved Jimmy hard, and

Jimmy went flying backwards, smashing into the wall behind him and crumpling to the ground. Jimmy felt the wind knocked out of him. The entire party was focused on the confrontation, but nobody moved.

    Sunny seemed to awaken from a trance as he observed what was happening. He stepped in between Jimmy and Ajay. "Boys, chill," he commanded. "This ain't between us." And then he spoke to Jimmy. "Take your boy home, then. It's clear outside now. We'll handle the business."

    Jimmy shook off Jenny, who was trying to help him to his feet. "I'm good. Thanks," muttered Jimmy as he stood up.

    Without another glance at anyone, Jimmy pushed Gary forwards to the door. He obliged without question. Jimmy could hear Ajay breathing heavily as they stepped out the basement door.

    Jimmy didn't utter a word to Gary as he drove away. They had noticed the gunshot holes in the house's garage as they walked to Jimmy's car, and this seemed to sober them both up.

    Jimmy pulled up to Gary's house, and there were a few seconds of silence as they both gazed out the window. "I'm sorry," Jimmy said softly. "For bringing you. I shouldn't have."

    Gary's eyes narrowed slightly as if he was concentrating on something. Then without a word, he opened the car door and headed inside. Jimmy sat there for a few moments after Gary had disappeared, his window cracked slightly open. The only sound came from the wind rustling against the trees. Other than that, silence enveloped Jimmy. He put his car back into drive and headed for home.

-15-

JIMMY AWOKE SUNDAY morning to his mind racing and his head pounding. He lay paralyzed in bed for a few hours, contemplating the ceiling and all that had transpired the previous night. When he finally rolled out of bed, he was immediately met with throbbing shoulders and a pulsating forehead. His jaw ached from clenching throughout his sleep, and his eyelids were heavy and sore. He felt defeated.

Something underneath the physical symptoms of the hangover felt much worse. It was a helplessness that he couldn't shake. He felt antsy and irritated and uncomfortable. A cloud of misery consumed him. An emotional hangover.

Jimmy saw that Sunny had texted him at 7 a.m., asking to meet up to blaze a joint when he woke up. Jimmy stared at the message for quite a while, recalling how the night had ended. Finally, he texted back that he would meet him in an hour at the cage.

It was a dreary, overcast afternoon when Jimmy pulled into the cage. The clouds threatened to unleash rain at any moment, and the world looked as depressed as Jimmy felt.

An awkward tension lingered in the air as Sunny sparked up a blunt. His shoulders were slouched, and he was leaning up against the cage fence as if it was keeping him from falling down. If it was possible, Sunny looked worse than Jimmy. He was wearing the same clothes from the previous night and clearly hadn't slept a wink.

"Listen Jimmy, I just want to say I'm sorry for how things went down last night."

Sunny hardly ever called him by his name. It was usually youngin or young buck or something similar, to remind Jimmy of his place.

Jimmy nodded but didn't offer a reply. He felt indifferent to the whole situation and distant towards Sunny.

Sunny took a deep drag of the blunt. Then another. "You got brains and you got balls," Sunny continued. "You were right last night when you said we should have waited 'til today to figure out what we were going to do. If I'd done that, then…"

Sunny's voice trailed off into an uncomfortable silence, and Jimmy knew something really bad had happened. Sunny's usual cocky demeanor had abandoned him and had been replaced with a sunken vulnerability.

Jimmy stared at his mentor and boss, who had schooled him in the ways of the game. The guy who had always warned him to be careful and calculated when making moves. The guy who had taught him to be cautious about using what he was selling. The guy who had told him the number one priority in this game was making money. Not retaliation, not girls, not anything else. It should always be about the money. Jimmy had appreciated these pearls of wisdom because they just made sense.

But as he stood there, looking at a shell of a man, Jimmy realized Sunny didn't abide by his own rules. He was a phony.

"I want you to know that I'm going to start trusting you more," Sunny continued.

"You're going to get the respect you deserve."

Jimmy nodded again and accepted the blunt that Sunny had finally passed to him. He took a deep drag and held the smoke in his lungs for as long as he could before opening his mouth and allowing the smoke to pour out of his mouth. They both watched the swirling cloud that had formed between them.

"The phones been blowing up," Sunny said. "I don't have it in me to see anyone. Work today and then take the rest of the week off if you want."

There was a tense silence as his request hung in the air. Just as Jimmy was about to respond, Sunny whispered, "Please. Whatever you make is yours. I won't take anything off the top." His voice had become soft and timid, as if he was pleading.

Jimmy stared at Sunny and knew he couldn't say no. It wasn't about the money or because he was scared of Sunny. Not in the slightest. It was because as Jimmy looked at Sunny, he didn't want him to be any more broken than he already was. But he knew that their relationship could never be the same.

"You got the stuff with you?" Jimmy finally answered.

Half an hour later, he was on the road with the product in his glove department and the phone on the passenger seat. He felt more relaxed after smoking the blunt. Weed could do magic, offering a way out of any fog you were in.

The phone vibrated, and after doing his customary scan of the road, Jimmy picked it up.

"Hello, good sir," a jolly voice from the other end bellowed.

Jimmy knew immediately that it was a guy he had secretly nicknamed Santa Claus. He had been one of Jimmy's first clients after starting to work Sunny's phone.

"Hey, whatup G?" Jimmy replied. "The usual O?"

"Yessir," the man replied jovially. "That's what I call good customer service."

"Haha, you know how it is," Jimmy said. "You at home?"

"Yup."

"Aight, I'll be there in five."

At the next red light, Jimmy pulled out an ounce of weed that would run the guy $160. Before putting it in the front cup holder, Jimmy tore off a few nugs and stuffed them in his pocket for later.

He appreciated the calls from customers that only wanted weed. He was more comfortable selling something that he knew. Weed was pure. It was natural. It was a herb grown from the earth. Jimmy enjoyed the smiling faces of his customers when he handed them their green. Sometimes, he felt like a doctor providing his patients with their medication.

Right when Jimmy pulled up to the man's house, the door opened. Out walked an older gentleman with an appearance that corresponded to his nickname. He was wearing a toque, but strands of his white hair were poking out from the side. He had a thick, white beard and plump cheeks and wore a button-down denim shirt with baggy jeans and sandals.

He approached the car, and when he saw it was Jimmy, his face brightened even more than usual. "I thought that was your voice," he said, smiling. He pulled out a folded piece of paper from his pocket, still grinning, and passed it to Jimmy.

"Haha, yeah. How you been? Haven't seen you in a minute." He unfolded the paper and saw it was the newspaper article about him.

"Amazing article about you, son. You should be very proud," Santa Claus said, leaning his head through the passenger side window.

"Thanks," Jimmy mumbled.

"You don't seem too enthused."

Jimmy framed a smile. "Ah, yeah, it's nice. But we still got some work to do. Trying to keep my head in the game."

Santa Claus nodded agreeably. "Very mature of you, son. Keep your eye on the prize."

Forcing out a laugh, Jimmy pulled the sack of weed from the cup holder and handed the weed and the article back to Santa Claus, who accepted it and gave Jimmy the cash. Before he turned to walk back to his house, his smile transformed into a serious expression. "I'm hoping that there will be a day I call, and it's not you answering the calls no more," Santa Claus said quietly. He waved the article gently in his hand. "This is what you should be doing. Not this." He motioned to the weed in his hand.

The sincerity in his voice sent shivers through Jimmy. "Thanks," was all Jimmy could muster. With that, Santa Claus nodded and headed back inside.

Night had fallen when Jimmy figured he would take one more call before quitting for the day. So when he got a call from a woman who lived in Whalley and asked for a gram of heroin, he obliged and began heading in that direction.

The address she gave him led him to a shabby four-story building that was used for low-income housing.

Jimmy had told her to be outside, but all he saw were a couple of scrawny guys leaning against the front of the building, smoking cigarettes. Jimmy redialed her number. No answer. He tried again. Still no answer.

Jimmy could see the two guys eyeing him down, and he felt tingles of anxiety. He was about to reverse out of the building parking lot and head back to Sunny's when his phone finally buzzed.

She seemed distraught and out of sorts as she managed a hello.

"Been downstairs for five minutes. About to leave," warned Jimmy.

"So sorry. I'm going to be just two minutes."

Jimmy could hear the distinct sounds of a baby crying in the background and a soft voice saying something right after, a voice that sounded like a child's.

"Be quiet," the woman snapped at the timid voice. "Go take care of your sister."

"Who's that?" Jimmy asked.

"I'll be just one minute. Coming down right now. Don't go," the woman pleaded.

Jimmy sat motionless, and watched a minute later as a woman rushed through the front door. She was wearing a light, pink robe and fluffy slippers to match. Her blonde hair was tied in a bun, revealing wrinkled, blemished skin. Bright red rashes lined the part of her arms that Jimmy could see, and she had what looked like cold sores all over her face. Judging by her facial structure, Jimmy would have guessed she had been attractive in her non-heroin years, but the drug had sapped her of her beauty.

"Thank you so much for waiting," she exclaimed as she rushed to the car.

Now that she was closer, Jimmy could see she had blue eyes that looked lifeless and worn, as if she had seen and done too much. Reluctantly, he pulled the bag of heroin from his cup holder. "We-were those your kids I could hear?" Jimmy stammered, hoping she would have some sort of rational explanation but knowing she wouldn't.

Her grateful expression immediately turned to anger. "Are you judging me?" she spat. She snatched the bag out of his limp hand and threw him the money. "Learn to do your fuckin' job." Then she turned around and stormed back inside. The two guys standing against the building began whispering to each other. One began to approach Jimmy's vehicle as the other guy trailed behind.

"Hey, you," one of the guys yelled.

Jimmy finally regained his senses and shifted his car to drive. He slammed his foot on the gas, staring at the men in his rear-view mirror as he sped away.

He didn't know what to think as he drove back to Sunny's. He knew the woman was right. Things like this came with the territory. If not from him, she would have gotten it from someone else. Compassion was not honoured on the streets. But he still couldn't shake the sound of the baby crying, and the soft little voice.

Suddenly, in his rear-view mirror, Jimmy saw a police car that was driving in the opposite direction pull a U-turn and flash on its siren. Jimmy looked in both mirrors, didn't see any other cars around him, and knew the sirens were directed at him.

Jimmy immediately began to panic and could feel his heart pounding through his shirt. The cop was still half a block away. He had sold quite a bit of product, but there was still plenty left in the glove department. Definitely enough to get him expelled from school and into some serious trouble.

He forced himself to take a deep breath and looked again in the rear-view mirror. The cop car was gaining distance on him, but Jimmy still had time. Without consciously deciding to do it, but knowing it was his only option, Jimmy slammed his foot on the gas pedal. He swerved right at the upcoming intersection, then tried to steady his nerves and figure out exactly where he was. There was a four-way stop sign at the next intersection. He knew he had to get through that four-way before the cop turned the other corner to follow him. Jimmy pressed on the gas pedal until he could feel it hit the floor. Without even looking to see whether there were cars coming in either direction, he busted a quick left at the stop sign, catching a glimpse of the cop just before his car was out of sight. Not taking any chances, he hung another quick right, then a left. He could hear the sound of the siren fading and eventually couldn't hear it at all. He knew the cop had lost pursuit.

Sweat was dripping down his face, but he could feel his heart rate gradually begin to slow down. He turned into a cul-de-sac and pulled over to the side, feeling a pulsing ache in his shoulders and neck that shot all the way up his skull and into his forehead. He felt lightheaded as he tried to take deep breaths to steady himself.

He'd never had a close call like that before. He knew that both Sunny and Ajay had been booked multiple times. Sunny had told him that run-ins with the police were inevitable. A slap on the wrist and then a delayed court case maybe a year down the road. Most of the time, the case would get thrown out, or you might have to do a few days of community service. It was a joke, Sunny had told him, and simply a by-product of the business they were in. Jimmy believed him and had thought he was prepared. But in that moment, he wasn't too sure of anything anymore. He hadn't been in quite some time.

Jimmy drove to Sunny's basement using side streets in case there was an alert on his car. He didn't mention anything to Sunny when he dropped off the phone and the rest of the product. He knew Sunny would praise his boldness if he told him. But Jimmy wasn't looking for praise. He wanted direction. He wasn't getting it at school. And now he knew he wasn't getting it from Sunny either.

-16-

JIMMY DIDN'T GO to school on Monday. He couldn't. His energy was at an all-time low, and he was questioning where his life should go. Everything he thought he knew didn't seem so real anymore. He had already known the answer didn't lie in a high school education, and now he knew he wouldn't find it on the streets either. He was lost in both directions.

Jimmy was lying in his bed on Monday evening when he heard his mom calling his name. "Jimmy," she yelled from downstairs. "Your friend is at the door."

He rolled out of bed and trudged downstairs. Mike was standing in the front entrance. "Whatup, G," Mike said, smiling.

Jimmy nodded without returning the smile. "Whatup, bro. What's going on?"

"Not much, man. Missed you at practice today. You sick or something?"

"Yeah, something like that."

From under the hallway light, Mike could see the deep bags under Jimmy's eyes. "Sullivan Heights won their first-round game, eh," Mike continued, changing the subject to something Jimmy might appreciate. "It's them we're up against on Friday."

Jimmy nodded. Even this news didn't excite him. He simply felt numb and wanted nothing more than to go back to his bed.

"Me and Gary are gonna hit up the mall right now. Try to get our mind off the game a little bit. You down to roll with?" Mike asked.

"Nah, I'm straight. You guys have fun, though."

"Come on, man," Mike persisted. "Gary has been on me all day to get you to come to the mall with us today. It'll be chill."

Jimmy eyed Mike suspiciously. "Gary wants me to come?"

"Yeah man. All day he's been asking."

Jimmy hesitated. He hadn't exchanged a word with Gary since Saturday night. He knew Gary had bumped lines of cocaine and probably popped a few pills. His glazed-over eyes as he'd agreed to whatever Ajay and Sunny were saying was implanted in Jimmy's memory. He should never have brought Gary to the party. Gary was like his little brother, and Jimmy had let him down.

"Aight, I'm down. Let's go."

They picked up Gary and headed to Metrotown, which was about a thirty-minute drive. During the car ride there, Jimmy felt himself relax, and it reminded him of simpler times when the most important thing in his life was basketball. He and Gary talked and laughed like nothing had happened.

Jimmy and Mike decided to visit Holt Renfrew first. Gary joined them, although his only indulgence at the mall was usually at the food court.

Sunny loved Holt Renfrew. Jimmy had joined him on one of his shopping expeditions just a few weeks prior. Sunny had brought a wad of cash and left with just change in his pocket.

As they entered the store, an attractive and well-maintained Hispanic man immediately greeted them. He had assisted Sunny the last time they were there.

"Jimmy," he said through a thick accent. "How nice to see you again."

"Ah, you remember my name. Very impressive," Jimmy replied casually.

"Of course, of course. What brings you in today?"

Jimmy took a scan around the store. He didn't really need anything urgently. "Just checking it out. Let me take a look. I'll holler at you if I need anything."

"Of course, you just let me know," the man said politely, offering Jimmy a slight bow before receding. Jimmy couldn't even remember his name. Maybe it was Juan. He looked like a Juan.

He found Mike and Gary admiring jackets in the Gucci section. Mike had pulled a black leather jacket from a hanger and was looking at it lovingly.

"I want this jacket so bad," Mike moaned.

"What's the issue, then? Just use Daddy's credit card," Jimmy joked.

"Ha, ha," Mike replied sarcastically. "I wish. No way they would let me. Look at the price tag."

He handed Jimmy the jacket. When the leather touched his fingers, it sent shivers up his spine. It had a rugged appearance, the way a leather jacket should have. But the material was smooth as Jimmy brushed his hands across it.

"Try it on," Mike said.

Jimmy slipped off his jacket and handed it to Gary. Right when he put it on, he knew the jacket was a perfect fit. He fixed the collar and looked in a nearby mirror.

"Dude, you look like a G," Mike said.

"Wow," he heard a familiar voice from behind him. "Amazing." Juan had returned, hand on hip and head tilted as he nodded approvingly.

"What you think, Gary?" Jimmy asked.

Gary had taken a seat off to the side, seemingly not as infatuated with the jacket as Mike or Juan. "Looks good," he said, standing up and smiling, but Jimmy could sense the indifference in his voice. "How much is it?"

Jimmy turned the sleeve over and found the price tag. His heart dropped. "Six hundred," he replied, trying to be casual.

Gary's mouth dropped. "Wow. That is insane." He shook his head in disbelief.

"Pshh, don't listen to Gary," Mike interrupted. "He wouldn't know fashion if it hit him over the head."

"It is made of the finest Danier leather," Juan said, seeming to want to contribute to the debate. "A classic. A jacket you can have in your wardrobe for years."

Jimmy paid no attention to Juan, knowing praise was his job, and instead directed his attention back to the mirror. Man, it did look good though, and he could feel the cash in the back pocket of his jeans.

In the reflection, he could see Mike almost drooling and Juan emphatically nodding with his phony smile. Jimmy's attention returned to Gary, who had the same disinterested look cemented on his face, as if he couldn't care less about anything in the store.

And then instantly, Jimmy recognized the insanity of the situation.

Here I am, willing to go broke to buy something I don't even need. This is the problem. Is this what I'm hustling for? Is this what I'm willing to get busted for? So I can buy shit like this and walk around like I'm the big man on the block? This is insane. People go broke for this shit.

He glanced around the store, and he knew he didn't belong here. Without another thought, he took the jacket off and handed it to Juan.

"I'm good, homie."

Juan looked severely disappointed as Jimmy exited the store.

After the usual contemplation and debate in the food court, they settled on Nando's. Mike and Jimmy both had wraps, and Gary ordered a half chicken to himself.

"So Sullivan Heights won," Jimmy said.

Mike nodded. Tamanawis had beaten Sullivan earlier on in the year by eighteen points. But Jimmy knew they couldn't be complacent. This was playoffs now. One loss and the Provincial Championships would escape their grasp.

"PM won their game too," Mike continued. "They beat King George by thirty. Arun Sandhu scored forty points and had twenty boards. The guy's a beast."

Jimmy went silent. He knew instinctively that another showdown with PM was inevitable. They were on opposite sides of their regional bracket, and only one of them would be able to earn a berth at the Provincials.

He was busy devouring his wrap when he looked up and saw Mike staring at him. It was obvious that Mike was contemplating something and deliberating whether he should bring it up.

"What up?" Jimmy said to Mike. "Don't worry, bro, I won't bite."

Mike grinned. "It's nothing, man. But Karen's been on me about it to talk to you."

Jimmy returned to eating his wrap. He knew what was coming next.

"It's Jessica," Mike continued. "She's been kind of a wreck since last week."

"Why? It was her that broke up with me."

"Come on, man. You know it's not like that. There ain't a person in this world that cares about you more than that girl."

Jimmy remained quiet. He had tried to persuade himself that his encounter with Jenny at Sunny's party was justified. After all, he and Jessica had broken up. But he couldn't escape the deep-seated guilt that would rear its head anytime he thought about Jenny. He knew he was entirely to blame. For everything. He just couldn't or wouldn't admit it.

"Just think about it, man," Mike persisted. "There ain't a guy in school that wouldn't do anything to be with Jess, but she's only got eyes for you, man. And you're mad because she just wants you to be a better version of yourself." Mike didn't make his point very politely, but Jimmy knew he deserved it.

"I'll keep that in mind," Jimmy replied.

After making his point, Mike excused himself to go to the washroom, leaving Jimmy and Gary by themselves. There was an uncomfortable silence as they both attempted to focus on their food and not what had to be talked about.

Gary spoke first. "Listen, Jimmy, I'm sorry. This weekend was my fault. I screwed up."

Jimmy looked at him, startled. "What you mean, man? That night was all on me. I shouldn't have left you alone for that long. Especially not with Ajay." Gary remained silent, so Jimmy continued. He had a lot of pent up things he'd been meaning to say.

"I know you were rolling on a few things that night, but that wasn't your fault. You didn't know anyone there, and I know you were already a bit anxious that night. I should have known better. And I just keep thinking about what would have happened if you would have went with them that night. I haven't been able to sleep, man. And now all this shit I've been doing with Sunny… I'm questioning everything, man. I don't know if I can keep doing it."

Gary's eyes shifted away from Jimmy, and it seemed like he was beginning to tear up. Gary took a deep breath to compose himself before he spoke. "Ajay hooked me up with a few bumps of white that night, and I think I had some molly too. But I still should have never volunteered to go with those guys. It was just in the heat of the moment, but I knew better. You standing up to Ajay like you did meant a lot to me."

And then Gary took a much deeper breath, as if he had his own confession to make. "Ajay texted me the day after. Didn't say much. Just that I was a down homie and I could link up anytime I wanted."

Jimmy's expression turned cold at Ajay's name. "What you tell him?" he asked quietly. He could hear Gary's leg bobbing with anxiety under the table.

"I just told him that I appreciated it. And that was it."

Jimmy glared at Gary and said, "He's bad news," not hiding the distaste he felt for Ajay. "You tell me if he hits you up again." Gary nodded. "I love you, bro," Jimmy said.

"You're my brother. If anything comes up—and I mean *anything*—you let me know."

"Love you too, bro. And I will for sure."

-17-

IT WAS THE Friday afternoon before their basketball game against Sullivan Heights, and Jimmy was sitting in Mr. Singh's math class. Mr. Singh was reviewing some algebraic equations that Jimmy could not follow in the slightest. He struggled to keep his drooping eyes open and resisted the urge to yawn loudly.

Mr. Singh's lecture was suddenly interrupted as the phone in his classroom began to ring. Jimmy used the opportunity to rest his forehead on the desk and give his eyes a break.

Why is it so much easier to sleep in class than at home in bed?

"Jimmy!" His head popped up off his desk as he heard Mr. Singh bark out his name. The teacher grinned. "You can nap after. Principal Nelson would like to see you in his office."

Jimmy quickly gathered up his things and could feel the eyes of his classmates glued to him. On the walk down to the office, Jimmy tried to figure out what Principal Nelson would want. He had an idea of what it might be, but he refused to believe it. They couldn't do that to him. Not a few hours before the game.

He knocked on Principal Nelson's door. "Come in," a voice responded. Jimmy opened the door and could immediately feel the somber energy that had attached itself to the office.

There were two chairs across from Principal Nelson's desk. Jimmy felt his heart sink as he saw one was occupied by Coach Dhillon.

Principal Nelson stood up when Jimmy entered. He was a short, stocky man and had a thin, pencil-lined goatee. He was mainly balding other than a few wispy strands of hair that clung to his scalp. His smile was jolly, and he had a hearty laugh that would bellow from deep in his belly.

Jimmy was quite fond of Principal Nelson, mainly because he was a big sports fan and seemed always to give Jimmy the benefit of the doubt.

"Have a seat, Jimmy," Principal Nelson said politely.

Jimmy tried to make eye contact with Coach Dhillon in the hope of receiving some sort of positive reinforcement. But the coach's eyes were fixed straight ahead as Jimmy took a seat beside him.

"Do you know why you're here?" Principal Nelson asked, maintaining his polite and even tone.

"Not quite, sir. I was hoping that maybe you were just going to wish me good luck on the big game tonight." Without even looking, Jimmy could feel Coach Dhillon clench up in his chair, and Jimmy knew what this meeting was about.

"Jimmy, I am aware that Coach Dhillon spoke with you a few weeks back. He informed you of some concerns that were brought forward regarding your attendance, attitude, and missed homework assignments. He also mentioned that there were two conditions that had to be met in order for you to continue to be a member of the basketball team."

Jimmy remained silent.

"I've had a chance to speak with both Mr. Pratt and a few of your teachers this week. Any idea what they would have told me?"

Jimmy shook his head. There was nothing he could say.

"Well, Mr. Pratt told me that he could not disclose the details of your meeting, as it was between just the two of you. He said you showed up, but he wouldn't tell me anything further. I asked him whether he thought you should be allowed to play. And he said yes."

Jimmy's heart felt like it had stopped. That was not the answer he was expecting.

And then Principal Nelson took a deep breath before continuing. "The issue is the conversation I had with your teachers, and your attendance record. I see multiple missed classes over the past few weeks. And I understand that you continue to not hand in homework assignments. Unless you have an explanation, I have no choice but to suspend you from the basketball team. Do you have an explanation?"

Principal Nelson allowed Jimmy a chance to respond, but he remained silent. All the hope and optimism he had felt a moment before was obliterated, and he felt nothing. Not sad or angry or disappointed. His mind felt like it shut off as he sat there in a daze. He didn't know what to think or what to say.

Principal Nelson continued to speak, but the words failed to register, and he noticed Jimmy's glazed-over expression. "Jimmy, are you okay?" he asked worriedly.

Jimmy didn't acknowledge the question. He continued to sit there, feeling utterly paralyzed.

"Have confidence in your team, Jimmy," Principal Nelson said. "If they win today, and you show initiative with your schoolwork and I get some positive feedback from your teachers, we can re-evaluate our decision for the next game. I hope you'll be there tonight to support your team."

Jimmy remained impassive, but he had found his voice. He knew if they lost today, there wouldn't be a next game. "Is there anything else, sir?" There was no resentment or bitterness in his tone.

"That is all, Jimmy," Principal Nelson replied, obviously still extremely concerned about Jimmy's reaction—or lack of one.

Jimmy stood up, and without glancing at Coach Dhillon or Principal Nelson, he left the office.

Math was his last class of the day, and he had no intention of going back for the last few minutes. He definitely didn't want to be around anyone after school either, so he headed straight for the exit.

When he got home, he took a shower and watched some TV, hoping to distract himself from what was going through his head. Halfway through a sitcom that he didn't find remotely funny, he heard his front door open as his dad returned from work.

When he entered the living room and saw Jimmy lying on the couch, he looked confused. "Shouldn't you be getting ready for the game, son?"

His dad was being polite, but Jimmy couldn't help but become irritated, so he didn't respond and instead turned up the volume on the TV. His dad stood there for a few seconds before retreating into the kitchen to talk to Jimmy's mom.

Soon after, Jimmy couldn't tolerate the TV any longer either, so he flipped it off and went to his room. The alarm clock on his desk flashed 5 p.m. His teammates would probably just be getting to the school to change and warm up. It wouldn't be long before Coach Dhillon would inform them that Jimmy wouldn't be playing. His heart hurt at the thought of letting his teammates down.

Suddenly, he felt extremely angry. Not with Principal Nelson or Coach Dhillon. Or Jessica or even Sunny. He was furious with himself. It was his fault. He was the one to blame.

He felt his hands clench into fists, and he had the urge to punch something hard. He resisted the temptation, instead collapsing onto his bed and putting his pillow over his face, trying to drown himself in darkness. But the darkness only proved to be a breeding ground for more destructive thoughts. He didn't know what to do.

He was out of weed and had no desire to call Sunny for some. He couldn't phone Jessica—he had messed that up. Gary and Mike were playing in the game right now, and even they wouldn't understand what he was going through. He had no one.

Jimmy settled on staring up at his ceiling, imagining how good it would feel if there was a massive earthquake and the drywall crumbled down, suffocating him. Finally, there would be some peace and quiet.

He knew he had to leave his room. And he knew where he wanted to go.

Despite it still being early February, the mild, snowless winter had continued. That afternoon had been mainly cloudy. As he had expected, the cage was empty when he pulled into the parking lot.

He unlocked the latch and stepped into his favourite arena. Unzipping his backpack carefully, without any haste, he pulled out his Spalding basketball. The grooves were smooth beneath his fingers. His eyes felt light as he gazed lovingly at the ball and the court. They could never take the game away from him.

First, he pounded the basketball against the pavement twenty times with his right hand, feeling each time it smacked up against his hand. He changed to his left hand and did the same thing. Then he walked the length of the court, crossing the ball over from left to right and then right to left, still pounding the ball as if he were trying to crack a hole in the pavement. Then he dribbled between his legs, changing speeds as he ran up the court.

After his dribbling drills, he worked on penetration and layups. He moved to different positions around the perimeter, visualizing how an opponent might try to defend him. Sometimes he would do a scoop layup, and sometimes it was a finger-roll, and he always made sure to practice with both hands. Drenched in sweat, he removed his sweatshirt and grabbed a water bottle from his backpack, paying no attention to the water that missed his mouth and splashed down his chin, onto his shirt. Refreshed, he tossed the bottle down beside his bag and went back to work.

For the next fifteen minutes, Jimmy worked on his cardio and conditioning. He began by running sprints. He would start at one side of the cage and run to the other side and back. Then he did defensive slides, crouching down into an athletic position and imagining an opponent trying to beat him off the dribble. Once he was done that, he did fifty burpees and a hundred push-ups. He finished off with shooting drills.

These drills were always saved for last, when he was exhausted and his legs felt like they could give out at any moment. The game didn't care about how tired you were. All it cared about was that you put in the work. In the fourth quarter, with the game on the line and when your arms felt heavy, Jimmy wanted to know that he had done everything to prepare. Fatigue wouldn't be the thing that defeated him.

By the time he made his final shot, he had removed his underarmour fleece shirt, leaving his undershirt as the only protection against the chilly, early evening breeze.

Jimmy kneeled over with his hands on his knees, staring down at the pavement. He felt the sweat pouring down his face and could see a small puddle forming at his feet. He knew that he was done and had nothing left to give.

He put his basketball against the caged fence and sat on it, slowly feeling his breath return to normal. He closed his eyes and enjoyed the wind against his face and the feeling of the cold steel against his back. Slowly, he opened his eyes and gazed around him.

It was beautiful. Beautifully ordinary. Nothing had changed from when he'd arrived an hour ago, but everything looked different. Different but the same.

The cluster of trees that stood just past the cage looked majestic in their noble presence. They hung in a group together as if they were best friends, their branches touching. The sky had turned a bluish grey as the sun departed and the moon emerged from its resting place.

He saw a seagull flying high above him. Its wings were stretched out wide, and it seemed to be flying in circles.

Where is it flying? Jimmy heard the voice in his head say. *Nowhere,* it answered.

It's just flying, because that's what birds do.

Jimmy wasn't sure whether it was the exhaustion from his workout, but in that moment, everything felt right. Suddenly, none of his problems seemed that important.

He sat on that basketball until he heard someone jiggling the latch. He calmly looked over and saw a boy who must have been around eight or nine, holding a basketball in one hand and looking frustrated as he tried to get the door open. Jimmy smiled as he stood up and walked over to unlatch the cage from the inside.

"Thanks," the boy chirped before running onto the court and heaving up a shot from the three-point line that fell a few feet short of the rim.

"Thanks," he heard another voice say from the door. It was a man in his early thirties who Jimmy assumed to be the boy's father. "He couldn't get here fast enough," the man said.

"No problem at all," Jimmy replied. "I know the feeling."

The man smiled at Jimmy. "It's a beautiful game."

Jimmy nodded before returning to pack up his bag. Thirty minutes later, he found himself parked inside the Tamanawis parking lot. The clock in his car read 7:52 p.m. The game would nearly be over. Cars crowded the lot, and he ended up having to park at the very far end. Jimmy stretched his neck from side to side and massaged the knots that had tightened in it. His stomach filled with angst about walking into the gymnasium and the possibility of seeing Tamanawis down on the scoreboard. And the hopeless feeling of knowing there was nothing he could do about it.

Jimmy walked to the school's back entrance, which was closest to the gym. When he got closer, he could begin to hear the sounds of the crowd, and he caught what sounded to be like a collective groan. His heart began to beat against his shirt.

The door leading into the gym was propped open. Jimmy took a deep breath and crept towards it. His heart seemed to stop as he peered up at the scoreboard: 61–59 for Tamanawis, with just over forty seconds remaining. Paul had just been fouled and awarded two free throws. While the teams were getting into position for the free throws, Jimmy surveyed the crowd.

He quickly found Jessica, who was sitting and cheering with Karen and a few of their other friends. And then as his eyes continued to dart from person to person, he saw someone looking directly back at him. Mr. Pratt's blue eyes seemed to sparkle, even in the distance. He offered Jimmy a small but polite nod. Jimmy felt himself return the nod and then turned his attention back to the game.

Swish. Paul made the first free throw. The referee collected the ball and passed it back to Paul. He took two dribbles and spun the ball in his hand. Swish. Tamanawis was up by four points.

Sullivan Heights inbounded the ball and raced up the court. They knew time was not on their side and they had to score quickly.

Their coach was screaming directions. They seemed to be in too much of a rush, as the point guard accepted a pick from the power forward and heaved up a three-pointer with Paul's hand right in his face. The basketball clanked off the rim, and Gary jumped up for the rebound. He quickly passed to Paul, who spun away from his defender to avoid the foul, then sprinted up the court as the seconds ticked away. By the time the Sullivan Heights team managed to foul Paul, just a dozen seconds remained. The Tamanawis crowd had gotten to their feet and was applauding.

Jimmy knew his team would be advancing to the next round and would need only one more victory to clinch a spot in the Provincial Championships. His heart began to beat more rapidly at the thought of that game. If PM won their next game, which Jimmy was confident they would do, it would be a rematch against their rival school, and he knew it wouldn't be friendly. If they were to win, he knew that he had to find a way to play.

He had no desire to stick around for the final few seconds of the game, preferring to leave unnoticed. Thankfully, the crowd had been so engaged in the basketball game that it might only have been Mr. Pratt who'd spotted him. Just as he turned to leave, his eyes instinctively found Jessica once more. This time, she was not cheering along with the rest. Her eyes were piercing into Jimmy's, almost daring him to come inside. But he couldn't face the chaos. At least not yet. He turned around and headed for home.

- 18 -

HE STAYED AWAY from everyone that weekend. Sunny had called him on Friday night after the game, and then again on Saturday afternoon when Jimmy still hadn't returned his call. Eventually, Jimmy turned his cell phone off and stashed it away in his backpack.

He knew he couldn't keep on going the way that he was. He saw dead ends in every direction. The only certainty in his life was that he wanted to play basketball.

His first class on Monday morning was English with Ms. Chohan. He got to class early, and when he walked in, he realized he was the first one there. Ms. Chohan was sitting at her desk, reviewing the outline for the class. She heard Jimmy enter and turned to face him.

"Hi, Jimmy. Nice to see you," she said politely and then returned her attention to the outline.

He remained at her desk, knowing there were unsaid words hanging in the air. "Ms. Chohan."

She placed the class outline in a folder on her desk and swiveled her chair around to give him her undivided attention. "Yes?"

"I just wanted to apologize for how I've been in class lately. I know you're just trying to help, and I appreciate that," Jimmy said.

"Thank you."

"And I'm going to do better," Jimmy continued. "I'm going to catch up on my assignments and all that. I just wanted to let you know."

Ms. Chohan seemed to deliberate carefully over her next few words as she eyed Jimmy somewhat suspiciously. "Show me with your actions," she finally said. "Words and promises can only take us so far." Jimmy nodded as he turned to take a seat. "And Jimmy," she continued. He turned towards her. "You had your appointment with Mr. Pratt, didn't you?" He nodded. "He's a wise man. Much wiser than me. Pay attention to what he says," she added before pulling the outline out again.

Jimmy took a seat at the front of the class rather than in the back corner, which was usually reserved for him. He looked again at Ms. Chohan, and all the animosity he had held towards her seemed to disappear. She had been raised differently than he was, and her beliefs were based on her own life experience. Just like his beliefs were based on his. Right and wrong wasn't ultimate. It was just based on a person's own conditioning.

When the bell rang after second period, signaling lunchtime, there was only one person that Jimmy was looking to find.

He stood several feet away, watching Jessica. Her locker was in the bottom row, and she was bending over slightly, just enough for Jimmy to see the small of her back.

Her long, brownish hair was tied in a ponytail, and Jimmy smiled when she brushed a piece of hair from her forehead. She was only wearing sweats and a hoodie, but he couldn't help but admire her figure. With Jessica still turned towards her locker, he approached her from behind. He tapped her shoulder, and she turned to look at him with her deep, penetrating eyes.

"Can we talk?" Jimmy asked softly. She hesitated for just a moment before nodding. "Do you want to go for a walk?"

"Sure," she replied as she finished putting her books away and closing her locker.

They were both silent as they walked, not sure exactly what to say. After a minute or so, they reached a wooded area just beyond the school grounds. They continued into the trees, and the further they walked, the further away everything else seemed to become.

Soon, there was no visual of the school, or the street, or any buildings at all. It was like they had left it all behind. Noise from the outside world slowly faded away. Although it was quiet, it was not an uncomfortable silence. There were birds chirping above. There was no way to know exactly where the voices were coming from, as the trees were evergreens, shielding the birds with their branches. But it didn't seem to matter. Their chirping sounded so in harmony with where they were, like it was the music of nature.

There was an open space among the trees, and Jimmy stopped, then turned to look at Jessica. "I'm sorry." She remained silent, so he continued. "The only thing that you've ever done is want the best for me and push me to be more than what I am. I've always recognized that, but it's just…"

He stopped and tried to articulate what kept him from living up to the expectations that everyone seemed to place upon him. "I don't know what it is. Sometimes, I just get so wrapped up in my own head, and I guess I lose sight of what's important. It's like my mind takes me in ten different directions, and I can't stop it."

Jessica was looking away from him towards the trees but now turned and concentrated on just him. "What is it that you want?"

Jimmy reached forward and took her hand. "I want you. And I want to play basketball. And I just want to enjoy these last few months of high school. Without all the bullshit and distractions."

He could sense her hesitation, as if she wanted to say something but resisted. She pulled her hand from Jimmy's grasp and walked a few steps away. "How about Sunny?"

"I got caught up in his game," he replied. "Way more than I would like to admit. It was never my intention to go as far with it as I did. But it was like when the ball started rolling, I couldn't stop it. I didn't want to let him down. Because I thought he had the answers to all my questions."

"And?" Jessica asked softly. "Did he?"

Jimmy laughed, almost to himself. "For a while, I was convinced that he did. But no, he didn't."

"How deep into it were you?"

He felt tingles of irritation in his stomach but knew that he had to get past it and be honest with her. "Everything you've heard is probably true. I mean, at first, it was easy enough to justify what I was doing in my head. All I was doing was selling weed to my boys and making a little bit of pocket money." He took a deep breath and contemplated the stillness of the nature surrounding him, sensing his body unclench slightly as he tried to convey to Jessica how he felt.

"By the end of it, though… Which is right now… I couldn't tolerate myself anymore. I was hustling a lot more than just weed. In my head, I convinced myself that these people were going to get the product from somebody else if not me. So what did it really matter? But it did matter. I was sacrificing everything else that was important in my life for this shit. None of the other stuff seemed to matter. Not basketball, not you, not my future. I could say it was the money, but it wasn't just that. I became what the game made me. It's time for me to move on. I'm gonna tell Sunny that I'm through."

As Jimmy uttered those final words, his shoulders began to feel lighter, as if a burden had been lifted from his back.

Jessica nodded. And then they both fell silent. He stared at Jessica, who was standing just a few feet away now, her back against a tree. He walked towards her slowly, not allowing his gaze to stray from hers. When he reached her, she looked up at him, and he knew that her heart was still with him.

He softly pushed her up against the bark of the tree, then grasped her hands, and they interlocked fingers. He leaned in for a slow, gentle kiss, waiting for her to accept his lips. When she did, he slipped his tongue into her mouth and felt hers meet his. Then he let go of her hands, moving them towards her hips and then around to her back, pulling her in closer.

When the kiss ended, their bodies remained connected as they gazed into each other's eyes. Jimmy could smell the lavender-like fragrance of her conditioner. He took a step back. With Jessica still leaning against the tree and partly out of breath, Jimmy looked her up and down seductively. She instinctively bit her lower lip as she tried to control her urge to kiss him again.

- 19 -

After the final bell rang, signaling the end of the school day, Jimmy knew there was one more visit he wanted to make before heading home.

He knocked on the door of the office he had visited just once before. A voice on the other side answered. "Come in."

Jimmy opened the door and took a step in. Mr. Pratt was leaning over his desk, packing up a few books into a black leather bag. When he saw Jimmy, he put the book he was holding onto his impressive mahogany desk and stood upright. "Jimmy," he said curiously. "Nice to see you. What brings you here?"

"I just wanted to apologize," Jimmy replied. Mr. Pratt's eyebrows seemed to arch slightly as he continued to look at Jimmy with a curious but interested expression. When he didn't immediately respond, Jimmy took a deep breath and tried to recall what it was he had come here to say. "I just wanted to apologize for storming out that day and saying some of the things I did. I was just in a bad place, and it was unfair for me to take it out on you. And I heard from Principal Nelson that you didn't tell him how things went down, and I appreciated that. It was just in the heat of the moment."

Mr. Pratt laid his leather bag down and walked towards the opposite side of the desk, nearest Jimmy. "Thank you for the apology, Jimmy. It takes a big man to admit when he is wrong. I know it's not the easiest thing to do."

"I've already delivered two apologies today. Hopefully this one is my last," Jimmy chuckled. Mr. Pratt smiled as well.

And then Jimmy frowned. There was something he had been wondering since the meeting in the principal's office. "Sir, I had a question for you," Jimmy said politely. "When Principal Nelson asked you if you thought I should be allowed to play in Friday's game, you said yes. You didn't have to say that, especially after how I treated you. Why did you?"

Mr. Pratt fixed his eyes on Jimmy's. His gaze was gentle and warm, as if he could smile with just his eyes. He walked slowly around Jimmy and towards the back of the room, reaching the gigantic bookshelf that wrapped around the wall. His attention was directed at some of the picture frames situated at the corners of each shelf. He located one and pulled it down.

Jimmy noticed how every movement Mr. Pratt made was never rushed, and how he seemed to take great care even when taking down that picture. Mr. Pratt returned to the front of the room where Jimmy was still standing and handed him the picture. It showed a young, muscular boy who looked to be around eighteen. He had long, shaggy hair and wore a jersey that said Canada on it. The boy was holding a basketball. He had a sharp jaw and well-defined facial features, much like the man who was standing in front of him.

"Is this you?" Jimmy asked incredulously.

Mr. Pratt laughed. "I guess you could say that. Although it feels like a lifetime ago."

"You played for Team Canada?" Jimmy looked up from the picture.

"Yes I did. Over forty years ago. When my knees didn't creak every time I stood up." He laughed again. "I didn't get much playing time. But I was playing with and against the best players in the world." Jimmy's shocked look did not escape him. "You look like you've just seen an alien," laughed Mr. Pratt.

"So why did you tell Principal Nelson that you thought I should play?"

"I said it because I know what basketball means to a kid who feels like everything else in his life has gone to shit. Because I was that kid. And basketball gave me a way out. At the very least, when I was out there playing, it finally felt like I was meant to do something."

Jimmy nodded. "The *Vancouver Sun* published an article about me a few weeks back." He wasn't certain why he was bringing it up, considering he hated when other people mentioned it to him.

"That's very impressive," Mr. Pratt stated.

Jimmy stared at his shoes. "You would think I should be happy about it, right?" Jimmy said. "But I'm not. I don't even know why, either. Sometimes, I don't understand much about why I feel the way I do. And I think that's the worst part. My mind just races, and it's like I have no control over it." He wasn't sure why he was telling these things to Mr. Pratt, who continued to look at him with an interested gaze as if he knew something Jimmy didn't.

"Are you planning on playing college basketball next year?" Mr. Pratt asked.

Jimmy paused, and his moment of hesitation provided Mr. Pratt with his answer. "Why not?"

"To be completely honest, I'd never even really considered it. I mean, I don't have the grades for it. And I know for certain that my parents can't afford to send me to college."

Mr. Pratt tilted his head to the side slightly. "You've never even thought about it?"

Jimmy realized that was a lie. He had thought about it, but he had never let his mind wander far enough to consider it a likely possibility. He was set on the fact that going to college was just a stepping stone to the inevitable eight-to-five grind that he'd promised himself he would never fall victim to. "I just don't think it's going to happen. Especially with all the stuff that's gone on lately. There's no way college coaches aren't going to hear about it."

Mr. Pratt nodded politely. At that point, his cell phone rang, and he excused himself as he stepped out of his office to answer it.

Jimmy walked to the back of the room, where Mr. Pratt had gotten the picture, and began to inspect the books in Mr. Pratt's collection. He remembered once taking pleasure in reading a good book. Before all the chaos that now permeated his life.

As Jimmy scanned the books, he noticed a wide range of all types of genres. However, one title in particular caught Jimmy's eye: *The Alchemist*. He removed it from the shelf and stared at it for a moment before hearing Mr. Pratt's voice.

"A fine selection."

Jimmy continued to stare at the book. "What's it about?"

"It's about a young boy who goes on a journey to find treasure that he is told is buried by the pyramids in Egypt. On a treacherous trek across the Sahara desert, he encounters many obstacles. But the most important obstacles that he's forced to endure are the ones right here," Mr. Pratt said, pointing to his head and then to his heart.

"Why is it called *The Alchemist*?"

Mr. Pratt paused. "Historically, alchemists were some of the wisest, most feared, and most respected men. They were supposedly able to transform base metals into pure gold. But in this book, it seems to have another meaning as well. The boy learns that the art of alchemy may also teach the way of transforming your dreams into reality. It suggests there is a beauty and grace that comes with following your intuition and your heart's true desires."

Jimmy nodded, looking down again at the book.

Mr. Pratt opened the top drawer in his desk and pulled out a file folder, then opened it and extracted a few sheets of paper. "Before our first meeting, I was reviewing your transcripts from the past few years," he said, looking down at the papers.

Jimmy suddenly felt a build-up of tension in his shoulders and neck. He tried moving his neck from side to side to loosen it up.

"It's quite remarkable, the drop-off that you've experienced from grade eight to now. In grades eight and nine, you had a very respectable GPA. And now... Well, I don't know what to think about your most recent transcript." Jimmy stared at the floor now, blaming himself for starting this entire conversation. "You don't enjoy talking about this, I can see," Mr. Pratt said.

"Nah, I really don't. I mean, what is there even to talk about?"

"Listen, Jimmy, if you don't want to talk about this anymore, we can drop it. But if you allow me to indulge you with my thoughts, maybe you'll find something useful in them. Would you like to hear what I have to say?"

Jimmy nodded. There was something about Mr. Pratt that intrigued him.

"I think you're scared," he said bluntly. Jimmy wanted to interrupt, but Mr. Pratt stopped him with, "Can I finish before you say anything?"

Jimmy gave a slight nod, although his face suggested disagreement with Mr. Pratt's statement.

"I don't think you're scared about anything that's happening out there," Mr. Pratt continued, pointing out his window. "You seem like a guy that can handle yourself verbally and physically. But in there, you're scared shitless," he said, pointing to Jimmy's heart. "And that fear comes from right here," he continued, now pointing to his head.

Jimmy felt the familiar pang in his stomach. "I'll put it like this Jimmy. Everyone you meet—classmate, teacher, CEO, or a drug addict on the street—has a voice going on inside their head. Most of these people have no control over what it is that their mind is saying. And to put it quite bluntly, most times, the voice in the head is nasty and conditioned by fear."

He understood precisely what Mr. Pratt was saying. The voice in his head played to the beat of its own drum, and Jimmy was just taken along for the ride. But he had simply accepted the fact that this was the reality of existence. Wasn't it?

Mr. Pratt smiled as he watched Jimmy trying to put the pieces together. His eyes twinkled. "Most times, you don't even realize that you're thinking this way, because it's so second nature to you. And over time, you build up patterns in your thought processes. These thought patterns dictate how we all live our lives. Some people have more positive thoughts than others. And others are more negative."

Jimmy nodded. "Yeah, I kind of get what you're trying to say. But that's just the way it is, isn't it?"

Mr. Pratt shrugged. "I don't know. The way I see it, there is something that transcends both negative and positive thought patterns. And it starts when you can start paying attention and hearing what's happening inside of you. You start to become connected to something deeper. The stronger this connection becomes, the more detached you become from these thought patterns. Their grip on you lessens, and your decisions become more conducive to your true purpose in life."

Jimmy went silent as he tried to comprehend. "I think I kind of understand," he finally said.

Mr. Pratt folded his hands on top of his desk and gazed into Jimmy's eyes. "I'll offer one more piece of advice, and then we'll call it a day. It's more of an experiment than a piece of advice. The next time you catch yourself stuck in your head, see if you can take a step back and observe the thoughts for what they are. Understand in that moment that the thought is happening within you, but it is not essential to you. Be the witness to your thoughts, and you'll realize more deeply who you are. You may experience a sense of detachment that you can't quite put into words. You certainly won't be able to understand it using your mind. It's more of a feeling than an understanding. You may find it easier to bring your focus to your breathing, which will automatically redirect attention from your mind."

Jimmy nodded. He knew there was truth to what Mr. Pratt was saying, but he still wasn't quite sure what to *think* of it all.

"Feel free to borrow it," Mr. Pratt said, pointing towards the book. "Books shouldn't merely collect dust."

Jimmy thanked him and left, book in hand.

-20-

SUNNY CALLED JIMMY a few more times during the week. Finally, Jimmy texted that he wasn't feeling well and would call him on the weekend. Sunny didn't reply.

He spent the week trying to catch up on as much homework as he could. The more missed assignments he completed, the more he realized how far behind he really was. But with each finished assignment came a sense of accomplishment as he shifted it to the side and began to work on the next one.

Friday evening came, and Jimmy and Jessica decided to go to a movie with Karen and Mike. Jessica could tell that Jimmy really wanted Gary to come, so she decided to ask Nicole, as Gary was interested in her.

Nicole was on the student council, along with Jessica and Karen, and they were more acquaintances than friends. She and Gary had danced at the winter formal back in December, but after Gary sent a few text messages that didn't get a reply, he had stopped trying.

Jimmy didn't know how she had done it or what she'd had to give up in return, but Jessica convinced Nicole to join them. Gary seemed surprised when Jimmy called and told him, but Jimmy could sense a hint of excitement in his voice.

After showering and changing, Jimmy drove to Jessica's house to pick her up. Waiting outside, he reached for his phone and called her.

"Hey," she answered cheerfully. "You here?"

"Yeah."

"Okay, I'll be right down." A few minutes later, her front door opened, and out walked Jess. She was wearing a black skirt that stopped a few inches above her knees, showcasing her long, athletic legs. She had on a white blouse that revealed just enough of her figure to have guys salivating at what was underneath. A silver necklace and pendant that Jimmy had bought her for Christmas sparkled a couple of inches below her neck. But what Jimmy could not stop looking at was her smile. It wasn't a fake smile, like most people wore. It was genuine, as if there was a sincere happiness flowing from her soul to her smile.

When she saw Jimmy, her face instantly lit up. He smiled back. She really was incredible.

"Hi-i-i!" she exclaimed when she opened the car door.

"Hey-y."

Once she got in, she leaned over and kissed him on the cheek. He put his hand on her leg and squeezed affectionately, then reversed out of her driveway and headed to the movie theatres.

They pulled up to Strawberry Hill Cinema, which was in a very central location and served as a meeting hub for a lot of the high school kids in the surrounding area. Mike, Karen, Gary, and Nicole were already there, standing by the entrance, when Jimmy and Jessica walked up.

"Took you guys long enough," Mike said.

Jimmy checked his watch: 8:15 p.m. "What are you talking about? Movie doesn't start for another thirty minutes."

"I know," Mike replied. "But we gotta hit up the arcade beforehand. Best part about being here."

Jimmy grinned. "Those arcades are for kids ten and under."

"Pshh. That ain't gonna stop me."

They walked inside the crowded movie theatre and towards

the arcade. Jimmy and Jessica stood off to the side as they observed their friends. "Looks like they're getting along. They look cute together," Jessica said, nodding towards Gary and Nicole.

Jimmy smiled. He wasn't sure cute would be the word he'd use. They were both extremely awkward. Gary towered over Nicole and yet had the goofiest grin on his face as he tried to teach Nicole how to play Mortal Kombat.

Nicole was cute in the geeky sort of way. Her jet-black hair was straight, parted in the middle, and hung down to her shoulders. She wore glasses, and her clothes were usually too baggy. She seemed surprisingly interested in the game and in Gary. She was laughing a little too much and a little too loudly. Jimmy knew Gary wasn't that funny.

Jessica was leaning up against Jimmy, and he had his arms wrapped around her waist. He bent forward as he nuzzled his nose against the side of her neck, where he knew she was sensitive. She moaned quietly but then quickly stood up and away from him. Grasping his hand, she dragged him towards their friends.

"Let's play... Unless you're scared I'll beat you." Jimmy laughed and followed her.

After they played a few of the racing games, which Jimmy *let* Jessica win, they headed out of the arcade to go watch the movie.

Mike and Karen had selected a horror/sci-fi film that starred Will Smith. Mike had pre-purchased the tickets and managed to get back-corner seats for all of them.

Jimmy took the seat against the wall and leaned his head up against it, suddenly feeling very tired. He put his arm around Jess, who rested her head against his chest.

The previews were just ending as his eyes suddenly began to feel very heavy. Unable to keep them open, he quietly dozed off. He was faintly aware of the sounds of the movie in the background but was so comfortable that he paid them no attention.

He could feel Jess nestled up to him, so when she nudged him, he nudged her lightly back. Jimmy felt a tickling sensation on his neck, and he slowly opened his eyes and saw it was Jess. She was kissing him lightly. He took a deep breath and indulged in the feeling. After a few seconds, she returned her head to his chest and reached over, grabbing his empty hand. She caressed it lightly with her own. Jimmy's hands were quite rough from constantly pounding the basketball on pavement, and the softness of hers sent shivers up his spine.

He looked over at Gary and saw he had his arm around Nicole, who was cuddled up against him. Jimmy smiled and whispered to Jess to look. She grinned softly but didn't say anything, then returned her attention back to silently stroking his hand.

Jimmy felt a surge of warmth enter him. His body felt light and calm, and completely relaxed. Despite the loud noise from the movie speakers, he felt his mind become still and silent. His breathing became deeply natural as he gave way to the sensation.

Without intending to do it, or understanding why he did, he leaned over and whispered in Jessica's ear, "I love you." He had never uttered those words to Jessica before.

She turned her head and met his gaze. Her eyes were both soft and intense, but unmistakably, they were also filled with love.

"I love you," she whispered back.

And then she rested her head back on Jimmy's chest. He was certain she could feel his heart pounding through his shirt.

When the movie finally ended, they hung out in their seats until the rest of the audience had dispersed. When it was empty, they finally stood up and headed towards the exit.

"What did you guys think?" Mike asked excitedly. "The ending was insane. Will Smith is a beast."

"So insane, man," Jimmy laughed, knowing that he had paid attention to maybe ten minutes of the two-hour movie.

Jessica grinned as she looked up at him. "Oh yeah? What was your favourite part?" Jimmy squeezed her side as she giggled.

Gary was walking a few feet ahead with Nicole. Jimmy chuckled to himself as he saw them holding hands.

They reached the main lobby of the movie theatre and were gathered around, about to say goodbye, when they heard a loud voice directed at them. "Oh look, it's the Tamanawis Pussycats."

Jimmy whirled around and saw Arun Sandhu from their rival school, Princess Margaret. He was surrounded by at least ten of his friends. "We're gonna give you guys a beat down when we play," Arun yelled.

The crowd in the lobby turned to look at them. "Fuckin' brown guys," Jimmy heard someone say from the crowd.

Arun and his crew walked closer to Jimmy. He recognized a handful of Arun's friends from PM's basketball team. A few of the others who weren't on the team had biceps bulging from their t-shirts and full tattoo sleeves.

"Take care of your business next game. And then yeah, we'll settle it," Jimmy replied coolly.

Arun approached Jimmy until he was only a few feet away. Jimmy could feel Jessica tense up as she held onto his arm. "What?" Arun sneered. "You scared right now?"

Arun's eyes were bloodshot, and even at this distance, Jimmy could smell alcohol on his breath.

Jimmy sensed Gary approach him from behind. "You got a problem?" he heard Gary say.

Arun turned his gaze from Jimmy to Gary, and then his lips curled into a smile. "Oh look, it's the fuckin' ogre," Arun spat. "Is that your girl?" he said, nodding towards Nicole. Gary didn't respond, so Arun continued. "What the hell is she doing with a donkey-ass-looking guy like you? She must be confused. But to be honest, she's not much of a looker herself."

Jimmy knew Gary would be turning red with anger. He put a hand on his friend's shoulder and turned him around. "It's not worth it," he said quietly.

"Your girl, on the other hand," Arun said to Jimmy. "I'd give it to her. She can come chill with a real G."

Jimmy could feel himself begin to get hot, and his heart rate increased. He took a breath to steady himself, and then he let go of Jessica's hand and walked calmly up to Arun, staring directly into his eyes. "I know you're upset that we're here with girls and you're here with a bunch of dicks," he said, loud enough so Arun's friends could hear. "So while I go take my girl home, why don't you all huddle around and jerk each other off."

Arun's face turned livid as he shoved Jimmy. "You better watch your mouth, bitch!" he screamed.

Luckily at that moment, a couple of cops entered the lobby. Someone must have told them that there was a commotion happening inside. Jimmy was inwardly relieved, knowing he, Gary, and Mike were outnumbered four to one.

Jimmy grasped Jessica's hand and led her outside. Mike, Gary, Nicole, and Karen followed. Everyone said a quick goodbye and then headed directly to their cars, not waiting for another encounter with the PM guys.

- 21 -

JIMMY LAY IN bed that evening with his mind racing. He knew he had to talk to Sunny and tell him he wanted out. The problem was that he couldn't help but play all the potential scenarios in his head. And they all happened to be negative.

Eventually, seeds of doubt entered his mind.

Am I even making the right decision? Maybe I'm being too hasty, and I should just tell Sunny I need to work less. If I work a shift or two here and there, that could be fine. And I could work during the day. Then I won't even have to deal with hustling the hard shit. It would just be weed. Like it was before.

Jimmy knew that would never work out. He either wanted in or wanted out. And he wanted out. The only thing keeping him from telling Sunny was fear.

His mind drifted off to Jessica, and he asked himself: Was he more scared of Sunny or of losing Jessica? Without a moment's hesitation, he knew the answer. And then another image entered his mind: the top of Jenny's head in Sunny's bathroom as he remembered his unfaithfulness.

I could never tell her. What would be the point of telling her anyways? It would do no good for anybody involved. I thought we were broken up. It didn't even mean anything.

While all of these thoughts were circulating through his mind, he noticed something else. It was like a still voice in the background. The voice was making no effort to consume his attention like his other thoughts did, but it was there. And without understanding how he did it, Jimmy's mind began to quiet, and the voice revealed its message.

Be the witness, was what it spoke. It was hardly audible, but Jimmy recognized the voice as Mr. Pratt's.

Suddenly, he felt a space around the thoughts, and he could sense a sort of detachment from the continuous voice inside his head. He allowed himself to relax into this indescribable space.

He felt a current of energy coursing through his body, running from his toes all the way up to the top of his head. He didn't fight the feeling as he closed his eyes. All he could feel was the energy.

His attention had left his mind, as he felt himself inhabit his body from the inside.

Jimmy's neck muscles, usually knotted with tension, began to relax, and he felt his jaw unclench.

With natural ease, his attention found his breath. He slowly began to inhale through his nose. No effort was exerted as he allowed the oxygen to slowly and comfortably fill up his body. When he felt the air reach down into his stomach, he opened his mouth and allowed the air to pour out as slowly as it had come in. The constant unease that sat in the pit of his stomach diminished after a few deep breaths.

Jimmy felt his mind wanting to wander again. He noticed his shoulder muscles begin to tighten and the pang in his stomach want to return. But this time, Jimmy felt like he had a choice. He knew that he could follow the thought and allow it to overtake his consciousness. But Jimmy chose to remain connected to the feeling that seemed to go much deeper than any thought. He stayed connected with his body.

And finally, as he was dozing off, eyes struggling to remain open, he understood.

Jimmy awoke to the sun shining through his blinds and down

onto his bed. He lay under his covers and enjoyed the breeze drifting through his open window. He could hear the sounds of birds chirping, nestled in a tree that sat on the border of their neighbours' yard, and the faint sounds of a car driving by.

But other than that, it was mainly silent. For the first time in quite a while, Jimmy hadn't awoken to the worries of his mind. He awoke to the sounds of reality. He felt a tingling sensation sear through his body. Without meaning to do it, he smiled. In that moment, he felt more alive than he had ever been, and the strange thing was—he had no idea why.

Jimmy turned on his side and looked at the alarm clock: 7:15 a.m. A usual Saturday morning typically meant that Jimmy would refuse to abandon the comfort of his bed until at least noon. But this morning, he felt refreshed, so he slipped the covers off and walked out to the washroom.

After brushing his teeth, he turned on the shower and let the water pour down onto his body. He turned the knob so that cold water began to rain down. It took a few seconds for his body to adapt to the briskness of the temperature. Each time his body began to adapt, he would turn the knob, making the water colder and colder until the knob wouldn't turn anymore. Sometimes, Jimmy would do this after a tough practice or to recover from a bad hangover. But today he did it simply because he wanted to feel the water.

When he finally turned off the water, he remained standing in the shower, letting the ceiling fan whistle in the background. He felt the water slowly evaporate from his body until he was dry enough to step out without needing his towel.

The mirror, usually fogged up after a long, hot shower, was clear. Jimmy placed his hands on the counter and gazed at his reflection. His mind was still quiet. Most times, he would rush through his morning routine, but today was different. He looked into his own eyes, and he heard himself speak.

"What the hell is going on?" Jimmy asked the image in the mirror. And then he grinned, the reflection reminding him of the boyish innocence he had lost somewhere along the way.

"Hey," Jimmy's mom said as he entered the kitchen. "I heard you get up early. I'm making breakfast. Sit, sit. It won't be long," she said.

"Thanks, Mom."

This wasn't the ordinary eggs and toast breakfast that Jimmy was accustomed to. He could hear the bacon and sausages sizzling in the frying pan and felt the rumblings in his stomach. He was starving.

Jimmy sat down at the kitchen table and observed his mom preparing his plate. He felt a wonderful sense of gratitude towards her in that moment and appreciated all that she had to put up with by having him as her son.

She put the overflowing plate in front of him. "Eat, eat!"

Jimmy didn't have to be told twice as he dug in and began to devour the food. His mom busied herself with the dishes. He saw from the corner of his eye that she was watching him eat, making sure he was enjoying it.

The traditional Indian woman got more satisfaction from feeding the men in her life than almost anything else. She took it as one of her responsibilities, just like the man's responsibility was to make sure there was a roof over their head and food in the fridge. Many Canadians might have considered it old school, but that's how it was. Jimmy knew that a lot of people were outraged at these defined roles. But the system worked, at least with his parents.

Once Jimmy's plate was wiped clean, his mom walked over to collect his plate. She was still beaming. "Good, good, you ate it all. You're still a growing boy. Is there anything else I can get for you?"

Jimmy smiled and shook his head. "I'm okay, Mom. Thanks, though. I'm just gonna go upstairs and finish some homework."

She looked surprised at the word homework but just nodded.

He went to his room and pulled out a pile of paper from his backpack, which were assignments he needed to complete. Without thinking about what he had to do, or how long it would take him, he just sat down and started working.

Feeling his hand starting to cramp, he looked up at his clock: 1:05 p.m. He had been working for four consecutive hours and hadn't even realized it. He looked down at his desk and the number of completed assignments. There were still a few more to go through, but he had surprised even himself with how much he could finish when he put his head down and just worked.

Jimmy ended up going to the gym and getting in a good workout. He had called Gary to come with him, but there was no answer. By five o'clock, Jimmy knew that it was time to go see Sunny and tell him he wanted out.

Without knowing exactly when it had happened, Jimmy realized that the peaceful state from the morning had departed. His mind had resumed its usual pattern of self-doubt and restlessness. Nonetheless, he got into his car and made his way over to Sunny's house.

Jimmy pulled up on the side of the road, looking out at Sunny's house. He saw Sunny's Benz and Ajay's Lexus parked a few meters ahead of him. And then he caught sight of another vehicle that was very familiar: Gary's old Honda Civic. Jimmy felt his heart rate instantly increase. What was Gary doing here?

Refusing to think about it too much, he stepped out of his car and strode deliberately to the basement. He knocked, then heard Ajay's deep, rough voice. "Who is it?"

"It's Jimmy." He heard some muffled voices coming from inside, but eventually the door opened, and he stepped inside.

Sunny was sitting on the couch and had some of his product on the table, next to the scale and some bags. Gary was sitting on the seat next to him, and it looked like Sunny was teaching him how it was done. Jimmy recalled when Sunny had first taught him. It seemed like a lifetime ago.

"Whatup, youngin," Sunny said without looking up.

Jimmy had not seen Sunny since the day after his party, when they had smoked a blunt. He remembered how fragile Sunny had appeared that day as he pleaded for Jimmy to work. Now, he stared at Sunny and knew the tough-guy façade had returned. The only difference was that Jimmy now knew it was phony.

"What are you doing here?" Jimmy said to Gary.

"You ain't gotta answer him, G," Ajay grunted from the opposite side of the room.

Jimmy acted as if he didn't hear Ajay and he continued to stare at Gary.

Unable to maintain eye contact, Gary looked towards the floor before replying. "I just came down to smoke one. That's it."

Jimmy didn't know what to say. He also knew now was not the time to have a heart-to-heart with Gary, so he redirected his attention to Sunny. "Can we talk?"

Sunny put one of the baggies to the side, then looked up, surveying Jimmy. Finally, he nodded. Sunny led him through the kitchen and into his bedroom, where he shut the door behind them.

"Whatup then?" Sunny said, none too politely.

"What's he doing here?" Jimmy said, motioning towards the living room.

Sunny chuckled. "You'll have to talk to Ajay 'bout that. He's taken a liking for the kid. They've been chillin."

Jimmy couldn't help but swallow the little bit of saliva that was left in his suddenly dry mouth. "Listen, Sunny, I appreciate what you've been doing for me. But it's not working for me no more. I gotta focus on other things right now. All this shit I've been doing is just a distraction."

Sunny glared at Jimmy. "So what? What you saying?"

"I want out. I wanna focus on school and ball. That's it." Now that he had said it, he didn't really care how Sunny was going to react. The worst was over.

Sunny's glare turned icy. "You think it's that easy?" Jimmy remained silent as Sunny contemplated what to do. "You know what ROI stands for?"

Jimmy shook his head.

"Return on investment," Sunny replied. "I've invested a lot in you. How you gonna pay me back?"

"Let's not go down that road, Sunny."

Then suddenly, as if a thought had occurred to him, Sunny grinned. "I'll tell you what, youngin. We'll make a trade. You for Gary. What you say? You cool with that?"

Jimmy's entire body clenched up, and he felt his hands curl into fists. He felt hatred boiling up to the surface, and he knew it wasn't going unnoticed.

"Chill out, lil man. You don't wanna get hurt now. It's just how the game goes. I had high expectations for you."

"I had high expectations for you too," Jimmy replied.

Sunny's eyes lit up with anger. "What the fuck does that mean?" he said, taking a step forward.

Jimmy remained rooted where he was standing and stared directly into Sunny's eyes. "You know exactly what I mean. I thought you were teaching me the game. But you don't even follow your own code."

Suddenly, Sunny turned away from him and he walked towards the corner of the room, kneeling down to his locked vault. Once it was open, he pulled something out, and then he turned back towards Jimmy.

Sunny was holding a revolver, and he lifted it up, pointing it straight at Jimmy. He felt his heart stop as he stared down the barrel of the gun. Sunny's eyes were cold and distant and consumed with hatred. Jimmy couldn't say anything, nor could he move. His entire body was paralyzed as he felt death staring him in the face.

After a few seconds, Sunny's mouth curled into a smile. He brought the gun down to his hip. "Why so scared?" he said sarcastically. "Thought you had ice in those veins." Jimmy remained silent. "Remember who you're talking to," Sunny continued. "I brought you in. I'll take you out just as fast. I'm as real as they come. Believe dat."

And then Sunny looked down at his watch. "What you still doin' here, then? Ain't you got homework to finish or some shit?" Sunny returned the gun to his vault as Jimmy left his room.

Jimmy didn't see Gary when he returned to the living room. He noticed that his shoes were still by the door and knew that he was probably conveniently in the washroom. Jimmy was getting ready to leave when he saw Sunny whisper something to Ajay.

As Jimmy opened the door to leave, Ajay said, loud enough to make sure Jimmy could hear, "Told you he was a little bitch."

- 22 -

JIMMY SAT IN Jessica's room as the rain poured buckets outside. They were working on a book report for *Hamlet* for Ms. Chohan's English class. It was the one assignment where anytime Jimmy would start, he would end up crumpling his paper in frustration and chucking it in the trash. Something about the play was extremely personal to Jimmy, but he just couldn't grasp what it was. He had reread it again last night.

"So tell me again what you think the play is about," Jessica said.

"It seems to me that it's about betrayal." Jessica smiled but didn't say anything. She waited for Jimmy to continue. "Anger... the desire for power... and I guess death."

Jessica nodded. "That's true. But go deeper. Is there anything else that you noticed? Even if it might not be obvious."

Jimmy became frustrated that Jessica continued to pursue the topic. But she could sense from his tone that he was holding something back. "I don't know. I think that's it. That's all I got from it, really."

"What else?" Jessica repeated calmly.

Jimmy had a sudden urge to slam his book shut and storm out if she wouldn't believe him. Before he did, he looked up into Jessica's hazel eyes, which were glaring directly at him. They were steady and unmoving, but they were quiet, and that calmed Jimmy down.

He knew there was something deeper when he read *Hamlet*.

He just couldn't quite put it into words. He searched and felt a wave of vulnerability wash over him. As he allowed the feeling to overtake him, his mind became still.

Jimmy moved his gaze to just over Jessica's shoulder, and then he spoke. When the words came, they were soft but deliberate, and it felt as if they came on their own, beyond his volition.

"It was about the prince. He had a big decision to make when his own uncle murdered his dad. Most of the play was him trying to figure out what he should do about it. And we all have big decisions in our lives, don't we? So I guess we can all relate in some ways to what the prince was going through. When I was reading it, I couldn't help but notice how he would constantly second-guess every decision he would think about making. He always focused on all the things that could go wrong. It was like he was torturing himself from within. Like he was a prisoner locked up in his own mind. I think that's what Shakespeare was on about when he wrote this play."

His gaze returned to Jessica's and it was obvious that she knew he was talking about more than just the play. "But I don't know," Jimmy said hurriedly. "That might be completely wrong."

She didn't say anything at first, and the silence seemed to go on for an eternity. He felt his leg begin to bob beneath the table.

"How can it be wrong," she finally said, "when that was how it made you feel?"

His hands were lying on Jessica's desk as she sat next to him. She reached over and put her hands on top of his. Her touch must have had a magical current, because it put Jimmy at ease. "Jimmy," she said, never breaking eye contact, "pay attention to your own truth. And you'll never be wrong."

Jimmy smiled. "Since when did you become so wise?"

"Oh, I don't know," Jessica said, flipping her hair and returning the smile.

That revelation seemed to spark something in Jimmy, and he spent the next hour scribbling his thoughts down on paper as quickly as he could.

His backpack was open on Jessica's bed, and *The Alchemist* was poking out. When he finally put his pen down and admired his work, he saw that Jessica was lying on her bed, reading the book.

"Sorry, it fell out of your bag. Since when did you read for fun?" Jessica asked.

Jimmy grinned. "There's a lot you don't know about me."

"Well then tell me," she said, sitting up onto her bed and closing the book.

He hadn't told her about his meetings with Mr. Pratt. There was something extremely personal about his connection with the counsellor, and Jimmy felt it would be tainted if he started to talk to people about it.

"You wanna know something about me?" he said, standing up from her desk chair. She nodded. "How about that you're the best thing in my life. And I want to be the best version of myself, so you can be with someone that you're proud of," Jimmy said meaning every word. He sat down on the bed as she remained silent. "And you want to know something else?" he whispered quietly. She nodded again. "You look so fuckin' good right now."

She smiled. Suddenly, she got up from her bed and walked towards her half-opened door. She peeked outside, then closed the door quietly and locked it.

Jimmy grinned. "How about your parents?"

Jessica shrugged as she walked slowly towards the bed, never taking her eyes off him. His mind went blank as she pushed him back and got on top of him.

– 23 –

It was Wednesday afternoon, and the final class of the day was English. Jimmy had enjoyed Ms. Chohan's shocked expression when he had handed her a stack of paper.

"My missed assignments," he had said.

Her surprise quickly turned into a warm smile. "I look forward to this."

In today's class, Ms. Chohan was talking about creative writing and different poets they had discussed over the course of the year.

"Shakespeare's messages were timeless and have spoken to the hearts of people over the span of many generations," Ms. Chohan said. "A true poet is someone who can make you feel things you already know in your depths but just have not discovered as reality yet."

Most of the class had one eye on the clock above her head, counting down the minutes. Ms. Chohan was not oblivious to this, so she posed a question.

"I want to hear from some of you now. What poet has had an influence on your life?" The classroom went silent as they pondered different poets that Ms. Chohan had assigned during the year. Some of them flipped through their notebooks—mainly to look busy so they would not be called upon.

Immediately, someone had come to Jimmy's mind. He surveyed the rest of the classroom, and no one had raised their hand, so he slowly raised his.

"Yes Jimmy," Ms. Chohan said.

"Nipsey Hussle," Jimmy replied. The class snickered, but Ms. Chohan stared directly at Jimmy without flinching. It seemed like she was trying to gauge whether Jimmy was joking or not.

"Care to elaborate?" she asked when Jimmy's face remained impassive.

"Well, you talk about Shakespeare and how his message was timeless and has meant so much to so many different people throughout the years. But it seems to me, like him and Nipsey are talking about the same things. Love, betrayal, revenge, death. They might say it in different words and in different ways, but the message is the same. Shakespeare doesn't touch my soul like Nipsey does."

"And what would you say to all of the profanity that he uses in his songs? Or when he talks about gangs, and guns, and violence. Or when he uses language to degrade women?" Ms. Chohan responded.

"The way I see it, the most important quality a poet can have is to be real. And I don't mean being real to the rest of the world. I mean being real to himself. To me, a poet is someone who can reach down into the dark basement of his soul that most people refuse to look, and confront the demons that they find. A poet is able to bring those feelings out as spoken words. What greater gift can there be in this world? To turn your feelings into words. And then to turn your words into art. If Nip writes about things that you or a sixty-year-old white guy can't understand, that isn't his problem. He's not rapping to you. He's rapping to me. He's rapping to those kids out there in the world that feel helpless and can't understand why they feel anger and discontent in the pit of their stomach. That's what a poet is."

Silence vibrated through the classroom. The bell rang, but everyone stayed seated. Jimmy had never spoken this much in class before. Most of the kids who knew him had classified him as the typical jock and part-time drug dealer who was too cool for school.

Ms. Chohan's expression had not changed throughout Jimmy's rant. Finally, her mouth curled into a smile. "That was amazing, Jimmy. I don't have to agree with what you said. But I do respect it. Enjoy the rest of your day, everyone."

As the students piled out of the classroom, Jimmy caught Ms. Chohan's eye. She smiled and nodded. He nodded back as he headed to basketball practice.

Jimmy still hadn't heard from Gary since seeing him at Sunny's, and he didn't see him at school the first few days of that week either. Gary also didn't show up to basketball practice. Jimmy was still permitted to practice with the team, although no one had officially told him about his status for the next game.

After Jimmy had showered and changed, he drove directly to Gary's house. If he wasn't going to answer his phone calls, Jimmy was going to find him and talk some sense into him. He was relieved to see Gary's car parked on the side of the road. After Jimmy parked his car behind Gary's, he walked around the side of the house and knocked on the basement door. From inside, he could hear Gary's mom yelling at Gary to answer the door. Gary must have not heard or obliged, because it was she who finally answered the door. Gary's mom was tall and slender and had traces of beauty that were masked by permanent bags that had formed under her eyes. And Jimmy couldn't remember ever seeing her wearing makeup. She was always too busy with something.

"Jimmy," she exclaimed. "How nice to see you. It's been too long. Come on in. Gary's in his room." She offered Jimmy something to eat and drink, but he could tell she was in a rush, so he politely declined.

She was frantically searching for something as she zoomed around their living room, looking under clothes scattered on the floor. There were unwashed dishes in the sink and pizza boxes and McDonald's paper bags on the living room table. With all the mess that littered the basement, it looked even smaller than usual.

"Sorry, honey, I can't find my keys. And I'm super late for work."

"Do you need some help?" offered Jimmy.

"That's okay. Gary's in his room. Oh, I already said that, didn't I? But I'm good. Thanks again."

Jimmy nodded and headed around the corner towards the rap music coming from Gary's room. He saw Gary's mom open the fridge and peer inside, as if her keys might be there.

The same trap music that Ajay and Sunny always listened to was blasting from Gary's bedroom as he knocked on the door.

"I'm busy," yelled Gary rudely from the other side of the door.

"It's Jimmy."

There was a brief silence before the door opened. Jimmy was disappointed not to be greeted by Gary's signature goofy smile. Instead, his face was serious and wore neither a frown nor a smile.

"What's up, man?" Gary said.

"Since when did you start listening to this music?" joked Jimmy, trying to break some of the tension hanging in the air.

"It's good shit, man," Gary replied.

Jimmy nodded. "Can we talk?" Gary's eyes narrowed slightly, but he eventually stepped aside to let Jimmy enter.

Gary's bedroom would be more accurately described as a cross between a big closet and a den. It barely fit a twin-size bed, and it had a small, cramped desk that hardly fit in the corner. There was a clothes rack pushed against the side, holding a few garments. Gary sat on his desk chair, and Jimmy took a seat on the edge of the bed.

"I didn't see you at school today," Jimmy asked. "Wanted to make sure you were okay."

"Yeah, I was a bit under the weather. Coach Dhillon called my mom today," grunted Gary. "I guess he wanted to make sure that I was actually sick. I think he just cares that I make it to school so I can play in our next game."

"It's a big game, man," Jimmy replied. "PM won. Arun dropped, like, forty. You're the only guy in this province who can stop him. It's gonna be us or them who make the Provincials."

Gary shrugged his shoulders as if he couldn't care less.

Jimmy wasn't used to the standoffish attitude from Gary, and he didn't like it. He knew Gary had probably been spending more time with Ajay than he had anticipated. "So what's the deal with you and Sunny and Ajay now?" Jimmy asked, cautiously but wanting to get to the point.

"We just chill once in a while. Blaze one," mumbled Gary.

Jimmy could feel himself getting more frustrated with Gary's lack of transparency. After all, they'd been best friends for as long as he could remember.

There was one question that Jimmy needed to ask, although he felt he already knew what the answer was going to be. He asked it anyways. "Has Sunny asked you to start working his line?"

Gary turned his chair around so he was facing the wall and away from Jimmy, which confirmed what Jimmy had thought.

"Fuck, man. Don't go down that path, G. It's dead ends in every direction. That shit is toxic."

This time, Gary swung his chair back around and glared at Jimmy. "How the hell can you say that? You've been hustlin' all this time, and I've always had your back. You never listened to me. What the hell makes it different now?" Jimmy stayed quiet. Gary had never blown up at him like that before. "Look at what I got, Jimmy. My mom is working her ass off for this shithole of a basement. And it ain't gonna get no better. I'm tired of being broke. It's either this or working fifty hours a week at some shitty fuckin' warehouse job once I graduate high school. Don't tell me you don't know the feeling."

"I get it," Jimmy replied. "But I've done it, and it ain't gonna lead nowhere. What's your plan, then? Hustle for some dough, and then what? You gonna do this forever? And Ajay and Sunny. Those guys are phonies."

Gary stood up from his chair and interlocked his hands behind his head. Jimmy could see that he was conflicted, but when he spoke, his voice was deep and angry. "You just sayin' that now because it didn't work out for you. I remember all the praise you used to talk 'bout Sunny. Something didn't go your way, and now you're just gonna lash out at him. That's pussy talk, man. Maybe it's time you take responsibility for your own shit."

Jimmy remained on the edge of the bed, stunned. He had expected the Gary he had known his entire life. The Gary who was always behind Jimmy's shoulder, ready to ride with him in any situation. Jimmy looked at his best friend, and he knew that he had lost him. Jimmy didn't say anything. He couldn't.

Gary had a pained expression on his face, and when he spoke, his voice was much softer, and all the resentment had left his tone. "You wanna be my boy?" Gary said.

"Let me figure this shit out on my own. Like I did for you."

- 24 -

JIMMY WAS CALLED back into Principal Nelson's office on Friday morning. This time when he entered the office, the energy felt almost the opposite to the first visit. Coach Dhillon and Principal Nelson were both present and had smiles plastered on their faces.

"How nice to see you, Jimmy. How are you doing?" Principal Nelson asked as Jimmy took a seat.

"Things are good. Just trying to keep my head down and focus on school, I guess." Jimmy did his best to maintain a neutral demeanor, not wanting to get his hopes up until he knew for certain why they had called him in. Thankfully, he didn't have to wait long.

"So we've heard," Principal Nelson continued. "We've spoken with your teachers, and they informed us that you've completed your missed assignments. And also that you've made a concerted effort to start participating in class."

Jimmy knew that Principal Nelson used the word "teachers" liberally, when "teacher" would have been more accurate. They all knew that Ms. Chohan had instigated Jimmy's suspension, and she was the one they had to go through to rescind it.

Jimmy felt the excitement building inside of him. No words came to his lips, but he felt his mouth curling into a huge smile. He turned to Coach Dhillon, who was smiling just as broadly.

"Let's get it," Coach Dhillon said to Jimmy.

"Yessir. Not gonna let the team down this time."

Principal Nelson spent the next few minutes explaining to Jimmy how he had an obligation to himself to excel, not only on the basketball court but also in the classroom. Previously, Jimmy would have zoned out when being lectured about how important a good education was. But this time, he did his best to focus on the message Principal Nelson was trying to make. As Jimmy left the office, he thought to himself that if nothing else, Principal Nelson genuinely wanted the best for him.

His good mood carried him all the way through the rest of the day and right into basketball practice after school. He was also pleased to see that Gary was present.

The team had gained confidence from their previous game, knowing they could still win without their captain and best player. No one had gained more confidence than Paul, who was enjoying the accolades from being the leading scorer in that game. Still, Jimmy knew that in PM, they would be facing a completely different animal. He hoped his teammates knew it too.

Coach Dhillon called the team in for a huddle. "We know that we got our game against PM next Tuesday. This is it, boys. This is the game to get into the big dance, like we've been waiting for all year long. We can't get complacent now. Let's make sure we play solid and play smart. Let's get in a scrimmage. Shirts and skins. Let's go."

The scrimmage was between the reserves and the starters. Gary won the jump ball and tipped it back to Jimmy, who dribbled up to the top left of the key and called out a play. He threw a bounce pass to Paul, then sprinted down to the paint to set a screen on Mike, who was supposed to curl around and receive the pass from Paul. Before Mike had a chance to accept the screen, Jimmy heard the ball hit the rim. He turned around and saw that Paul had taken a quick shot before the play had a chance to develop.

Jimmy remained silent as he ran back on defense.

The reserves missed a lay-up on their next possession, and Gary rebounded the ball and threw an outlet pass to Paul, who penetrated down the court. The reserves did a good job of getting back on defense, and Jimmy could see that the paint was clogged as he jogged up the floor. However, instead of pulling the ball out and waiting for his teammates to get into position, Paul drove the ball into the key and was met by a swarm of defenders. He threw up a wild shot and then stumbled to the ground.

"Foul," Paul yelled.

Coach Dhillon called a stop to the play. "Don't think that would be called a foul, Paul. It was just a bad shot," he said.

Paul didn't say anything as he got to his feet and walked back on defense, shaking his head.

All the chemistry he and Jimmy had built up over the season had become non-existent. There was an awkward tension between them, and it manifested itself on the court.

By the end of the scrimmage, the reserves had beaten the starters. "What the fuck we doin' out there!" Jimmy said as they walked back to the bench following the scrimmage.

"Don't worry 'bout us," Paul replied. "We show up every game, and we got the W last game. You might not remember 'cause you weren't even there."

"You got a fuckin' problem?" challenged Jimmy.

"Yeah, I'm lookin' at it right now."

Jimmy walked right up to Paul until they were face to face. "Well maybe you should work on that jump shot instead of crushing on my girl."

Paul turned beet red. He had no response, so instead he shoved Jimmy in the chest, making him take a few steps back. Mike quickly jumped in between them.

"Boys, chill. We're teammates."

Gary was sitting on the bench, seeming to have no interest in the confrontation.

Jimmy stormed into the change room, refusing to give him or anyone else another glance.

– 25 –

It seemed like the entire school was talking about the game. Because Tamanawis had finished first in their division, it would also be a home game. Jimmy couldn't count how many of his classmates stopped him in the hallway and wished him luck. This was the game to get into the big dance.

The entire year, Jimmy had been waiting for a game like this. A game that actually meant something and where the stakes would be at their highest. But now that it was finally here, his mind wouldn't stop considering all the things that could go wrong. He also couldn't shake the deep sense of responsibility for introducing Gary to Sunny and Ajay.

So Monday at lunch, Jimmy snuck away from his usual crew, hoping to speak with someone who could offer him some clarity.

Jimmy knocked on the door, hoping he was there. After a few moments of irritating silence, a voice emanated: "Come in."

Jimmy opened the door and entered Mr. Pratt's office.

The counsellor had his feet kicked up onto his desk, and he was leaning back in his reclining chair, holding a book.

"Jimmy," he said putting the book down. "How nice to see you."

"Hello, sir," Jimmy replied.

"Have a seat," Mr. Pratt said politely.

Jimmy obliged, putting his backpack on the floor and sitting down.

Mr. Pratt surveyed him intently, seemingly trying to get a read. "So how's the book?" he asked finally.

Jimmy paused, almost forgetting what book Mr. Pratt was referring to. "It's good. I'm really enjoying it."

Mr. Pratt scanned him again with curious eyes. "You haven't read much of it, have you?"

Jimmy smiled and shook his head. "I've just been so busy with everything else, and trying to catch up with school, that I haven't had much time."

Mr. Pratt smiled and nodded. "So what brings you in today? To the best of my knowledge, none of your teachers have requested that you see me."

Jimmy hesitated. He wasn't entirely sure how to explain what he was feeling. Somewhere, deeper than the surface, it was clear and obvious, yet he could not describe it. Words simply seemed like a cheap substitute.

Mr. Pratt waited patiently.

"When we met last time, you asked me to do something," Jimmy finally said.

"Read the book?" Mr. Pratt asked, laughing.

Jimmy shook his head. "You told me that when my mind started racing, and I couldn't get it to stop, to try to observe what was happening inside of my head and to understand they were just thoughts, and then to breathe through it."

The counsellor's smile transformed into an interested gaze as he waited for Jimmy to continue. "Well, it happened," Jimmy said, recalling that previous Saturday morning, when he'd felt that indescribable peace. "All this shit was happening in my life, and my mind felt like it would never shut off. But then, one night... I remembered what you had told me about being able to watch my thoughts. It was like from one moment to the next, the thoughts didn't carry as much weight anymore. They weren't that heavy. Everything became so clear, and it was like I understood but I couldn't put it into words. But I didn't *want* to put it into words. All I wanted was… I just wanted it to…" Jimmy paused, not knowing what it was that he wanted. The feeling seemed like a distant dream.

"To last forever," Mr. Pratt said quietly.

Jimmy looked at Mr. Pratt, whose face had remained calm. But now, his eyes were penetrating.

Jimmy nodded. "I was scared for the feeling to go away."

"And then what happened?"

"Real life happened," Jimmy replied. "I was involved in some stuff that I had to find a way out of. And it wasn't easy."

Mr. Pratt didn't nod, or even offer Jimmy a sympathetic smile. He simply stared at Jimmy with a blank expression, seemingly in deep contemplation about his response. "Does this have anything to do with Sunny?" he finally asked. Jimmy's body suddenly tensed up as he looked at Mr. Pratt in disbelief. "Some of your teachers had expressed their concern over your relationship with him."

Jimmy knew this could only mean Ms. Chohan. "How do you know him?" Jimmy asked.

"He went to Tamanawis, as you know. And we met in similar circumstances to how I met you. Let's just say he wasn't as open as you were."

Jimmy nodded. "For the longest time, I wanted to be like Sunny," Jimmy heard himself say. "I wanted to talk like him, walk like him, and act like him. It just seemed to me like he had the blueprint to be self-made."

Mr. Pratt chuckled. "Sunny isn't self-made. His dad is one of the biggest real estate developers in all of Surrey. He owns properties all over the city."

"Really? He never mentioned that."

"Well, I'm sure the story of being self-made sounds a lot better. I remember when Sunny was getting into trouble in grade twelve. I would try calling his parents. They were so caught up in their own lives and their businesses that I wasn't even sure whether they remembered they had a son. They showered him with gifts, and I guess they thought that was enough."

Jimmy couldn't believe it. Didn't want to believe it. Yet he wasn't surprised in the slightest. "Crazy," he muttered to himself.

"What is it that you want from me, Jimmy?"

Jimmy stared at Mr. Pratt like he should already know. How could he not? "I want all these voices in my head to stop. But they won't. They just run through every bad scenario that could possibly happen. And it's worse now. Because I know the voices *can* stop. I still remember the feeling when they do. But the harder I try to get back to that feeling, it's like the more I get stuck. I'm just tired of all the shit happening inside of me."

The counsellor didn't immediately reply as he continued to survey Jimmy, the way a curious cat might watch its human. "You have a big game tomorrow night, don't you." It was a statement rather than a question, as the whole school practically throbbed with the upcoming match.

Jimmy nodded. Mr. Pratt stood up and walked around his desk. Jimmy had forgotten how tall he was. He ended up at the back bookshelf, and he picked up the picture where he was wearing the Team Canada jersey. He looked at it calmly and attentively for a few moments, then put it down as gently as he had picked it up and turned back to Jimmy. "Why do you love the game?"

"That's easy," Jimmy replied. "The game has always been my escape from everything else. Ever since I was young, when I needed a distraction, I would pick up the ball and head to a hoop."

"I understand." Mr. Pratt didn't seem to completely accept his answer. "But what is it about the actual game that you love?"

There were a few moments of silence as Jimmy contemplated his question more deeply. "I love being great at something. I feel free on the basketball court." Another pause. "It's what I've always done. What I've always known," he finished.

Mr. Pratt nodded. "What else?" Jimmy didn't know what answer he was looking for. "Close your eyes. Don't overthink it. What do you love about the game itself?"

Jimmy closed his eyes, and he felt his mind begin to quiet. Instinctively, his attention went to his breath. He noticed how shallow and tense it was. Slowly, it became deeper and more even. Mr. Pratt's window was cracked open, and Jimmy could hear the faint sounds coming from outside. His attention went to the noises, but not just those outside. He followed the sounds of each thought inside his head. With the attention came the clarity. With the clarity came the silence.

"Why do you love the game?" he heard Mr. Pratt ask again.

This time he didn't think about it. He simply knew. "I love pounding the basketball on the pavement and feeling the ball each time it hits my hand. Or after a jump shot, when the basketball soars off my fingertips and I already know the result. I love the sound of a swish, when the ball doesn't even graze the rim. I love being bent over with my hands on my knees and sweat pouring down my face, knowing that this is exactly what I am supposed to be doing at this moment. But I think what I love most of all… is just the feeling of the basketball in my hands."

Jimmy slowly opened his eyes, and Mr. Pratt was standing there, grinning. He had a basketball in his hand and passed it to Jimmy.

"I can't tell you how to shut your mind off," Mr. Pratt said, "because the answer, the truth, is already inside of you. You'll have to discover it yourself."

Jimmy nodded. In the deepest sense, he already knew this.

"But I can offer you some advice about your game tomorrow. It was something I used to do," Mr. Pratt continued. "Whenever I began to feel nervous or tense or anxious about a big game, I came back to that feeling you just described. Not the thought, but the feeling. When you feel like you can't get out of your head, redirect your attention to that ball in your hand. That ball has a magic that defies logic. So don't think about the game. Feel the basketball. It has a tangible reality. Thoughts are just images in your mind."

Jimmy went quiet, letting Mr. Pratt's words sink in.

"And Jimmy. Just remember. Wednesday, when you wake up—win or lose, life goes on."

26

TUESDAY NIGHT HAD finally arrived, and Jimmy was in his room, packing his bag. He did this very carefully, making sure not to rush anything. He knew what tonight's game meant, and he wanted to appreciate every moment of the entire process. Win or lose, he refused to take this game for granted.

After placing his basketball shoes at the very top, he zipped up his bag and set it softly on top of his bed. Then he sat down next to it and picked up the basketball that Mr. Pratt had given to him.

A few years back, Jimmy had purchased a painted portrait of his two favourite rappers embracing—Tupac Shakur and Nipsey Hussle. This was the centerpiece in Jimmy's room, placed in the middle of the bare wall opposite his bed. It was impossible to not see it when he woke up or when he lay down in bed. Jimmy remembered buying it and bringing it home; initially, he would stare at it for hours at a time. But over the past year, he had simply overlooked it, letting it become familiar, allowing the ebbing of its allure.

But as he sat down on his bed now, spinning the basketball in his hands, he really gave it his full attention. He noticed how the artist had painted the picture with care and precision, sparing not a single detail. Both of the rappers had since passed away, but in that moment, they came alive to Jimmy. The humour in their smiles, the conviction in their eyes, and the aura of love that emanated from their beings were beautifully portrayed. Jimmy knew that the painter must have really loved creating art.

He stopped spinning the basketball and simply looked at it. Maybe that's what he was doing when he was on the basketball court. Maybe this was his way of creating art. He had never thought about it like that before, but what was he doing, if not that? The basketball court was his canvas, and he was the paintbrush. He would never be in the NBA, like he used to dream of as a kid, but that didn't matter. What mattered was he had a canvas. And he wanted to get lost in the art.

There was a nervous tension hanging in the air of the locker room before the game. Mike had gone out to take a peek into the gymnasium and had come back looking pale, telling the team he had never seen the bleachers so full.

The locker room, usually full of chatter and horsing around, had mainly gone quiet. The confident swagger of their previous games had dissipated, replaced by an anxious energy.

Coach Dhillon walked in, and it was obvious he could sense the nervousness in the room. He asked the team to huddle around.

"Boys," he said, trying to make eye contact with each of them, "I know how you must be feeling. For some of you, in your senior year, you know what this game means. This might be your final game playing competitive basketball."

Without even looking, Jimmy could feel some of the boys in the locker room tense up.

"And I know that you might not like to hear that, but it's the truth. We can't run from our demons. We have to stand tall and confront them. I want you all to do me a favour," Coach Dhillon said. "I want you to remember why you first started playing basketball. Everyone in this locker room shares at least one thing in common. And that is the love of the game. If you can recall that feeling, I want you to bring it out today when you're out on that floor. We know that we're the better team.

We just have to forget all the other distractions and go out and play our game."

Coach Dhillon curled his hand up in a fist and held it up to the ceiling. Jimmy stood up to join Coach Dhillon, and the rest of the team followed.

"Family on three," shouted Jimmy.

"One. Two. Three. Family!" they all yelled.

They sprinted out into the gymnasium to the applause and cheers of their home crowd. Jimmy looked out and couldn't see any empty seats in the entire bleachers. He scanned the crowd until he found Jessica. He had given her his away jersey to wear. When he finally caught her eye, she beamed a smile at him. He winked and gave her a little wave.

He also saw his parents in the bleachers. His mom, who was usually very quiet and reserved around other people, was on her feet, cheering. His dad and Inder had two large McDonald's cups. Jimmy smiled to himself, knowing they were probably full of Crown and Coke.

Jimmy caught sight of some of the other guys who had graduated last year from the basketball team. He also saw Santa Claus, who looked as jolly as ever. Quite a few of Tamanawis' teachers had come to the game to show their support; he saw Ms. Chohan, Mr. Singh, and Mr. Pratt. Mr. Pratt gave Jimmy a small nod when he caught his eye.

There was a section of the crowd that was full of PM students and parents. They were attempting to yell just as loud for their team, but the Tamanawis crowd drowned their cheers out. Jimmy scanned the PM section until he found her, like he knew he would.

Jenny was in the middle of the PM crowd, eyes glued to Jimmy. When she saw him looking, she smiled. He pretended not to see her and brought his attention back to the warm-up. He had one task tonight. Nothing else mattered.

After the warm-up, Jimmy felt revved to go. The butterflies in his stomach seemed to have transformed themselves into a fire ready to be unleashed.

Prior to tip-off, both teams usually shook hands. But when the teams congregated around the middle of the floor, all Jimmy saw was menacing glares. He stared right back, making sure they knew he was not intimidated in the slightest. He wished he could say the same about his teammates, but they were avoiding eye contact. The PM team had advanced this far into the playoffs not only because of their skill but also because of their physicality. They were known for bullying their way to victory.

Arun won the jump ball and directed the ball back to Karn, PM's shooting guard. PM passed the ball around the three-point line until there was an opening, and they fed the ball to Arun deep on the right block. Arun took two dribbles with Gary on his back, faked going right, and then turned to his left for a fadeaway jump shot. The ball hit the backboard and dropped into the net for the first points of the game. The PM crowd cheered.

Jimmy called out Tamanawis' first play of the game. The ball got to Gary on the inside, and he made a weak move against Arun towards the middle of the key. As soon as he put the ball on the ground, Arun reached forward and tipped it away. Arun collected the ball and then threw an outlet pass to Karn, who sprinted up the floor, making a crossover move on Paul before laying the ball in.

Jimmy took a deep breath as he walked up the court.

Paul curled around a screen set by Gary on the next play down. Jimmy took one dribble away from his defender and fired a pass to Paul, whose defender had stuck on his hip. Paul rose up and took a contested three-point shot. Jimmy could only watch as the ball soared a foot short of the rim and bounced out of bounds.

PM hit a three-pointer of their own on their next possession down, and then Gary missed another lay-up. After two converted free throws by Arun, PM had taken an early 9-0 lead.

Coach Dhillon called a timeout, and as both teams were walking towards their benches, Arun yelled out to Jimmy. "Tell your girl I say whatup. I'll hit her up after this beatdown."

Coach Dhillon spoke some words of encouragement that no one really paid attention to. But Jimmy's ears perked up when he heard his name.

"Let's try to get Jimmy the ball and let him do some work," Coach Dhillon said.

"And then let's feed off that."

Jimmy stood at the bottom right of the key after the timeout, looking up at the scoreboard and the big, fat 0 by Tamanawis.

Paul called out the play, and Gary ran to set an off-ball screen for Jimmy. He used the screen, and Arun switched off Gary to defend Jimmy. Mike set a second screen for Jimmy, who curled off that one and found himself wide open at the top of the three-point arc. He caught the pass from Paul and rose up in one sequence. The three-pointer was nothing but net. Tamanawis had finally put their first points on the board.

The PM guards continued to feed the ball to the inside for the remainder of the first half. Arun was exposing the Tamanawis forwards, and Gary appeared to be simply going through the motions.

On offense, Paul and the rest of the starters were playing tight, as if fearful of making a mistake. They began to pass up wide-open shots and look to pass the ball to Jimmy on every possession.

Near the end of the first half, Arun backed Gary all the way down to the bottom of the key, did a quick spin move, and dunked the ball home. As he ran back down the floor, he flexed his arm as if to tell Gary that he couldn't guard him.

Jimmy called an isolation play after he saw only eighteen seconds remained in the first half. PM was ahead 48–33.

Jimmy signaled for Gary to set a screen. Arun followed Gary up to the top, where Jimmy used the pick to force PM to swap defenders and now had Arun guarding him.

Jimmy pounded the ball against the floor as he stared up into Arun's eyes. He quickly penetrated hard to the right as Arun struggled to beat him to the spot. At the last second, Jimmy pulled the ball back and crossed it over to his left hand. Arun tripped over his feet and stumbled to the ground. Jimmy was left wide open at the three-point line and he rose up, letting the ball soar off his fingertips.

Swish.

Cheers from the crowd echoed through the gym as the buzzer signalled the end of the first half.

"We're only down twelve points, gentlemen. A couple buckets and it will feel like nothing," Coach Dhillon addressed his team in the locker room. "We can't lose our composure now. We've worked too hard this season to let up. We're going to switch up our defensive scheme and go into a 2-3 zone," he continued. "I want three defenders in the paint at all times. And if Arun touches the ball, I want someone from the top to come down and double immediately. If they want to beat us by making open threes, so be it. But no more easy buckets on the inside."

The horn buzzed from the gym, indicating five minutes until the second half.

All the time Coach Dhillon was speaking, Jimmy sat in the corner, head leaned up against the lockers and eyes closed.

As his teammates stood up to head back into the gym, Jimmy knew there were words hanging in his throat. "Boys," he said quietly.

The few teammates who heard turned around to face him. The rest of the team, realizing that Jimmy was speaking, now retreated back.

"We're getting stomped right now. And to be honest, this might be it for us. I know we've been taught that winning is the most important thing. I've stressed that more than anyone here. But I ain't going back out onto that court looking at the scoreboard. I'm goin' out there to play the game like I did when I was a kid. When just playing the game was enough. Let's let the score take care of itself. Let's go out there and bring the fight."

Paul approached where Jimmy was sitting. He held his hand out, and Jimmy took it as Paul helped him up to his feet.

"Let's do it," Paul said.

When they returned to the floor, the crowd rose to their feet in applause.

As his teammates began to warm up, Jimmy stood off to the side, holding a basketball in his hands. He kept his head down, allowing the cheers to sound like static in the background.

He looked up and gazed around the gym, and then he felt it.

He felt how a warrior must have felt when he stepped onto the battlefield. When it was him and the adversary, and only one could prevail.

He felt the inevitability of the fight, yet sensed the underlying calm underneath. He felt the urge to win, yet knew accepting defeat was the purest victory.

Jimmy continued to look around the gym and began to notice things that he usually overlooked.

He observed the light beams shining from above, and how one of them was dimmer than the others. His eyes surveyed the walls that had been painted a glorious blue, and the basketball hoops that appeared to be suspended in the air.

And then, finally, his attention returned to the basketball in his hands. He felt the energy in his hands become one with the ball as he caressed it gently. His fingertips began to tingle, and the feeling flowed into his hands and then the rest of his body.

He took a few hard dribbles and then joined his team for the final few minutes before the second half started.

On Tamanawis' first possession, Paul brought the ball up the floor and passed to Jimmy, who was at the top of the three-point line. Immediately, Paul's defender left him and sprinted towards Jimmy with his hands outstretched, trying to cause Jimmy to panic. But he coolly took two dribbles backwards and made a slick bounce pass in between the two defenders to a wide-open Paul, who couldn't believe he was so wide open and so he hesitated before shooting. The ball bounced off the front rim and was rebounded by Arun.

As they were running back on defense, Jimmy yelled to Paul, "All good, brotha. Keep shooting. They're gonna start falling."

On the opposite side of the floor, PM was not expecting the zone defense that Tamanawis had implemented. They looked out of sorts as they tried to find a hole in the 2-3 zone. When they couldn't get the ball into the inside, they settled for an open shot. It clanged off the rim and was rebounded by Gary, who threw an outlet pass to Jimmy.

He sprinted up the floor before PM had a chance to set their defense. He zigzagged his way through two defenders, leaving only one between him and the hoop. From the corner of his eye, he saw Paul running only a few feet behind him. Jimmy penetrated hard at the defender, who took a few steps backwards. Jimmy turned around mid-stride and handed the ball off to Paul, who was able to convert an easy lay-up.

"Atta boy," Jimmy shouted at Paul, slapping him on the behind as they ran back on defense.

It seemed like PM had also made an adjustment to their defense, as they began to double-team Jimmy whenever he touched the ball. As the half went on, anytime Jimmy saw a second defender coming towards him, he would look for Paul. It didn't take long for Paul to establish his own rhythm.

After a three-pointer by Paul, and with PM's lead cut down to only seven, the PM coaches called a timeout.

On the ensuing possession, Karn trotted off to the bottom corner of the three-point line. He kneeled over and put his hands on his shorts, looking lazily at his shoes. Jimmy instinctively knew Karn was trying to make it seem like he was a decoy and would not be involved in the play.

Arun trudged over and set a blindside screen on Jimmy, but he was prepared and was able to sidestep it. Karn reached towards the pass as he curled around the screen, but Jimmy was in perfect position as he tipped the ball and it trickled loose towards the half-court line. Jimmy raced after it, collected the ball, and saw no one between him and the basket. He sprinted towards the hoop, sensing the blood pumping through his veins. He jumped up to finger roll the ball into the hoop, feeling his adrenaline propel him higher, and he found himself in the air with the ball a foot above the rim. Jimmy dunked the ball home, and the crowd rose up and cheered.

With sweat pouring down his face, Jimmy glanced up at the scoreboard and it now read 73–68 for PM with only five minutes remaining.

"That's how we do it, boys!" Jimmy could hear Paul yelling.

The PM guards passed the ball at the top of the key, looking lost against the zone defense. The passes became predictable, and Paul was able to lunge forward and deflect a lazy pass from Karn. Paul ran down the open floor, prepared to lay the ball in. Karn sprinted after him, and from where Jimmy was standing, he could see the anger and frustration in Karn's eyes. When Paul jumped forward to convert the lay-up, Karn lowered his shoulder and laid a thunderous body check to Paul's stomach without making a play on the basketball. Paul's body slammed against the wall and collapsed to the floor. Jimmy was the fastest of his Tamanawis teammates, so he was the first to confront Karn.

"What the fuck was that?" Jimmy yelled, inches from his face. Jimmy was about to shove him when he felt someone pull him back by his shoulders. He turned around to find it was Gary.

"Not worth it, bro. Let's get this W," Gary said.

The fact that Gary, who was usually the first to be involved in a scuffle, was telling Jimmy to calm down woke him up. He nodded, and they both went to assist Paul, who was now sitting up against the wall. He seemed winded but okay other than that.

The referee issued a flagrant foul to Karn, which resulted in two free throws and the ball for Tamanawis. Paul made one of the free throws, cutting the PM lead to just four.

Mike inbounded the basketball to Jimmy, who turned away from the hoop, shielding the ball and waiting for the double team to approach. When it didn't, he turned back towards Karn, who was defending him. He took two hard dribbles to his right, then penetrated towards the hoop. Karn tried to cut off Jimmy, who crossed the ball over to his left, leaving Karn on his heels. Jimmy took three dribbles into the paint and saw the defense collapse in towards him. He spotted Mike open at the corner of the three-point line. Jimmy made an overhand pass to Mike, who caught the ball and launched up a three-point shot.

Before Jimmy even saw whether the ball had gone into the hoop, Arun, who could feel Jimmy on his hip, held his elbows up and spun towards Jimmy. The elbow connected squarely on

Jimmy's nose. He felt shooting pain all through his skull as he sprawled to the floor. Jimmy felt his eyes well up with water immediately. Opening his eyes, he saw blood spurting out of his nose.

He managed to lie on his side and could feel the commotion around him. Jimmy's vision was still blurry, but he could see and hear both teams yelling and pushing each other. He saw Paul and Mike trying to restrain Gary.

Gary broke free of their grip and stormed towards Arun. His eyes were bloodshot, and anger lined his face. Arun shook free of his coach's grip when he saw Gary heading towards him. Arun hesitated and tried to say something to Gary, but Gary was on him before he could get the second word out of his mouth. Gary grabbed him by the collar, wound up, and delivered a thunderous punch that landed flush on his face. Arun's knees buckled as he hit the floor. He seemed to be unconscious, as he lay there motionless.

This finally seemed to stop the commotion, as the PM players rushed off to attend to their teammate. Jimmy managed to get to his feet, although blood was still pouring from his nose. Someone handed him a towel, and he held it to his face to stop the bleeding. The gymnasium seemed to be spinning as Jimmy's teammates helped him to the bench.

Arun appeared to have regained consciousness and was being led off by a pair of his teammates into the locker room.

The referees, who had finally regained control of the situation, called both coaches into the centre.

Jimmy felt dizzy, but the bleeding seemed to have stopped. He wiped off the remnants of blood from his upper lip and chin. Looking up at the crowd, he saw Jessica, who was looking in his direction. Even from this distance, Jimmy could tell she looked distraught. He gave her a thumbs up, and she forced out a smile.

The entire crowd seemed to be in a frenzy as they talked about what had just happened. As Jimmy tried to steady himself, he gazed out into the bleachers and saw someone he hadn't noticed before: Sunny.

He was sitting in a back corner with Ajay. They were laughing, seeming to have enjoyed what had just transpired. Sunny caught Jimmy looking in his direction, and he leaned forward and whispered something into Ajay's ear. Jimmy turned away and tried to refocus on the game.

Coach Dhillon walked back to the bench and said something to Gary who still hadn't sat down. He was glaring at the PM bench, almost daring someone to step to him. After Coach Dhillon spoke to him, Gary turned around and walked towards Jimmy. He held out a closed fist.

"You good brah?" he asked Jimmy.

"I'm straight. Appreciate the backup," Jimmy replied.

"We're brothers. You know I always got you." With that, he walked directly into the locker room.

Coach Dhillon asked his team to take a seat on the bench before kneeling down in front of them. "Gary and Arun have both been ejected. The referees just gave PM and us a very strict warning. Another altercation, and the initiating team will forfeit the game." Coach Dhillon looked up at the scoreboard. "We're down four, but we still got two minutes remaining. Let's get in some quality possessions."

Jimmy threw the towel on the ground and stood up, prepared to re-enter the game. He felt himself wobble on the spot and knew he was still feeling the effects of the elbow. Coach Dhillon was staring at him.

"Have a seat, Jimmy."

"Coach, I'm good," Jimmy said, exasperated.

"You're still leaking from your nose," Coach Dhillon said, looking at his bloodstained jersey. "And you might have a concussion. The referees say you have to get checked out."

Jimmy reluctantly sat back down as the first-aid attendant approached him and began her tests.

As soon as she pointed a flashlight into Jimmy's eyes, he had to turn away. The light felt like it was blinding him and was followed by a sharp pain that seemed to stab at his brain. He closed his eyes, which gave him some relief, but this sequence was not missed by Coach Dhillon. Jimmy knew he wouldn't be allowed to re-enter the game.

He felt helpless as he watched his team struggle to make up the points they were down. *Have I played the last competitive basketball of my life?* Jimmy struggled to keep these thoughts out of his mind, holding onto faith that somehow, his team could make up the points.

After Mike missed a contested twelve-foot jump shot and Karn was able to convert on a three-point play, Jimmy felt the game slipping away. Tamanawis was unable to get any closer, and he could only watch as the final few seconds ticked away on the scoreboard, and on their season.

As PM began their celebration, Jimmy looked at the crowd, towards Jessica, and he felt his heart stop. Jessica was leaning her head back as Sunny whispered something in her ear.

-27-

JIMMY SAT QUIETLY in the corner of the locker room, feeling a wave of frustration and disbelief that it had ended like this. He was certain the result would have been different if he could have finished the game.

The locker room was eerily silent, with the only sounds coming from outside, where the crowd was filing out of the gymnasium. Coach Dhillon was the only one standing, and he was walking from player to player, whispering something to each of them.

When he reached Jimmy, he kneeled down in front of him and placed his hand on Jimmy's shoulder. "You left it all out there, son. And I couldn't be more proud of you. I just want to say how much I appreciated being able to coach you. And learn from you. You're a warrior all the way to your core. And I hope with all of my heart that this is not the last time I see you on the basketball court. That would be the only real loss."

Jimmy looked up at his coach, a man he had gotten to know over the past five years, and felt nothing but genuine love. Some of his teammates labeled Coach Dhillon too meek and too kind, but Jimmy would refute that. Coach Dhillon simply was who he was: a compassionate soul who truly cared about the welfare of his players and students. Jimmy nodded, and they both knew the love was mutual.

He then stood up and approached Paul, who had tears streaming down his cheeks. "You left it all out there, bro," Jimmy said.

Paul nodded but seemed unable to speak. "I feel it too," Jimmy said about the pain that he knew was in Paul's heart. They embraced, and that was enough.

Soon after, the rest of the team began to share hugs and reflect on what the last five years had meant to them. Some were speaking more than others, and no one felt ashamed to let their tears fall. For a lot of them, this was the greatest loss they had experienced up to this point.

Gary had already had time to change back into his street clothes and had an ice pack sitting next to him. Jimmy could see that Gary was choosing not to involve himself in the emotional camaraderie.

Jimmy walked up to him as Gary flung his backpack over his shoulders and repositioned the ice pack on his punching hand.

"Bro, you good?" Jimmy asked.

Gary looked up, and his face was impassive and indifferent. He forced out a small smile when he saw Jimmy. "I'm good, bro. How you feeling?"

"I'm good, man," Jimmy replied.

"Hit me up tomorrow or something. We'll blaze one," Gary said over his shoulder as he made his way to the door.

When they finally left the locker room and went outside to the parking lot, Jimmy was shocked to see how many people had remained, still scattered throughout the parking lot. Jimmy could feel hands patting him on the back with words of encouragement, and he muttered as many thanks as he could.

Jimmy found his parents and Inder, who were huddled together with some of the Tamanawis' teachers. Jimmy's dad and Inder were laughing and talking animatedly with Mr. Pratt and Ms. Chohan, and Jimmy could only smile. He definitely knew they had a few drinks in their system.

They turned to Jimmy when they saw him approaching. "You guys fought hard out there," Jimmy's dad said. "You should be proud."

"Thanks, Pops," were the only words that Jimmy could find.

Mr. Pratt was a presence in the crowd. He was a head taller than most of the other people, and he had a wonderful and peaceful vibration about him. He was standing a little off to the side, quietly observing everything that was happening. Jimmy caught his gaze. Mr. Pratt smiled gently, his blue eyes somehow twinkling in the dark of the night. "Brilliant game," he said.

"Thanks, but it still hurts." Jimmy paused as he tried to find some words to convey how he felt.

Mr. Pratt put his hand on Jimmy's shoulder, and Jimmy felt a chill shoot down his spine, as if the touch contained an electric current. "Well then let it hurt." Jimmy nodded.

He was scanning the crowd, trying to find Jessica, when he saw Gary's head above many others. Jimmy lifted up on his tiptoes to see who he was talking to. Gary was nodding emphatically with his goofy smile as Sunny said something to him. Ajay was standing close by.

Jimmy walked over to them. When Sunny saw him approaching, he stopped talking to Gary, leaned back, and said something to Ajay.

"Whatup, boys," Jimmy said when he reached them, making every attempt to keep his voice casual.

"Sup, young buck," Sunny said. Ajay remained quiet, but Jimmy could feel his glare.

"Thanks for coming out," Jimmy said.

"You know how it is," Sunny said, putting his arm around Gary. "We support our own."

Gary suddenly looked uncomfortable, as Jimmy stayed silent and surveyed the situation.

"So how's life living like a broke bitch?" Sunny asked.

Jimmy knew Sunny was trying to get a reaction from him.

"No problems. All I wanted was to come over and say whatup. That's it." Jimmy turned to Gary. "I'll see you tomorrow at school."

Then, as Jimmy turned to walk away, Sunny decided to throw another punch—and this time, he went for the knockout. "So Gary's been telling me that you're going good with your girl. Jessica right?"

Jimmy stopped in his tracks, and he knew what was coming next.

"I heard 'bout what happened at my place. In the washroom. It would be a shame if your girl found out."

Jimmy felt his heart pumping adrenaline as he spun around and stormed up to Sunny. He wanted to yell something at him. Instead, he felt himself take a breath, then whispered, low enough so only Sunny could hear: "By the way, homie, I heard about your trust fund from mommy and daddy. They pay for your car too?"

Jimmy didn't know how much of that was true, and he didn't care. He just wanted to cause a reaction. And it worked. Sunny's face became contorted as he racked his mind to think of an insult to hurl back. When he couldn't, Jimmy just snickered. "That's what I thought," Jimmy said. "Phony."

Jimmy knew that he shouldn't have said it. He could have just walked away. But he didn't care anymore. He felt hatred boiling in his soul, and he wanted to make sure that Sunny knew.

Sunny shoved Jimmy as hard as he could. There was a car parked behind him, and Jimmy slammed into the front bumper as his body fell back. The alarm started to howl. The entire crowd looked over to see what the commotion was, and they saw Jimmy slumped over the front of the car as Sunny advanced towards him.

"You know who I fuckin' am?" Sunny screamed at Jimmy. "You know what I've done, bitch? I'll end you."

Gary tried to rush forward to step between Sunny and Jimmy, but Ajay stopped him. "He deserves it. Walking out on Sunny like he did," Ajay said to Gary. "Let them settle it."

Jimmy had no energy for a fight. He was exhausted from the game, and the effects of Arun's elbow continued to linger. But Sunny didn't care. His hands were curled into fists as he reached Jimmy, who pushed himself up off the car and tried to prepare for what was coming. Before he could, Sunny wound up and punched him in the liver. It sent Jimmy to his knees. He was doubled over, trying to catch his breath, when Sunny kicked him in his ribs, and he collapsed flat onto the ground. Jimmy turned on his back and stared up at Sunny.

Jimmy could faintly hear people yelling in the background, but it was as if his senses weren't working properly. Sounds were muffled, and his vision was hazy. Through the fog, Sunny's face came into focus. His eyes were dark and glazed over, like a demon staring down.

Sunny was panting heavily, as if he had no control over his actions. Jimmy looked up at him blankly, and he saw what the physical manifestation of hatred looked like. He knew that Sunny's hatred went deeper than simply being directed at him. It was lodged in his soul.

As Sunny wound his leg back again to deliver another kick, Jimmy knew where he was aiming. He cradled his head with his arms to protect himself, shut his eyes, and braced for the impact.

But it never came. After a few seconds, Jimmy lowered his arms and looked up.

Mr. Pratt had Sunny in a headlock and had pressed him up against the car.

"Let go of me, bitch! You're dead!" yelled Sunny as he flailed his arms around.

But Mr. Pratt refused to release his grip. Jimmy's senses finally seemed to have returned, and it was as if they'd been turned up to full blast. There was a crowd around him, and he lost sight of Mr. Pratt and Sunny.

"Are you okay?" Jimmy heard from what seemed to be in ten different directions.

"Someone call an ambulance," he heard someone else yell out from the crowd.

Jimmy managed to sit up. "No, no, don't call an ambulance. I'm all good."

His mom and Ms. Chohan kneeled down beside him and asked where it hurt. "Everywhere," Jimmy chuckled. He noticed that his voice was hoarse, and when he laughed, he felt a pain in his ribs.

Ms. Chohan couldn't help but smile, and Jimmy's mom grasped his hand and squeezed with a strength that he'd never known she had.

"Where's Jess?" Jimmy struggled to say.

People were looking to their left and right, trying to locate her, but she didn't seem to be anywhere. Finally, her head poked through the crowd. Her eyes were red, and tears were streaming down her face. She looked distraught, and she hesitated before approaching Jimmy. "Are you okay?" she said through muffled sobs.

Jimmy looked at her and knew something else was wrong. Before he could say anything, he heard ambulance sirens.

"Just rest," he heard his mom say. He laid his head back down onto the pavement and stared up at the nighttime sky.

The darkness was vast and seemed to stretch on forever and ever. Chaos was happening all around him, but he felt strangely at peace. The sky seemed to go on in every direction, and the space of it consumed him. It didn't seem, though, to be outside of him. He was part of it. Or more accurately, *he was it*. He closed his eyes as the sounds of the sirens got closer and closer until they finally stopped. And then, all that was left was the stillness of the night.

- 28 -

THEY RAN A few different tests on Jimmy when he was at the hospital. He was diagnosed with a concussion, but the rest of the tests came back negative. In the end, the doctor told Jimmy and his parents that the best treatment would be rest.

His parents wanted to get the police involved, but Jimmy urged them not to. "It's going to cause more problems than it'll solve," he told them. "This is the end of it." His mom was not overly convinced, but she decided to drop the subject and let him rest.

As he lay in bed, his mind went through all that had happened that night. The loss, the fight, Jessica. The most difficult part was knowing there was nothing he could do about it.

Jimmy heard his phone buzzing from a text message just after 2 a.m. It was from Gary. "You up?" it read.

Jimmy thought something might be wrong, so he immediately texted back. "Yeah, what's up?"

"Nothing, just cruising around. Is it cool if I stop by? Have to get some things off my chest."

"Yeah, come down. I'm up."

Fifteen minutes later, his phone buzzed again, and Gary told him he was at the front door. Jimmy struggled to his feet, his body seeming to ache in every place possible, then slowly and quietly walked downstairs to not wake his mom.

When Jimmy opened the door, he did not see Gary's familiar goofy face. He hadn't seen it in a while. Rather, his face was sombre and his eyes looked weary, as if he had been beaten by exhaustion. Jimmy looked down at his hand, still swollen from the punch he had landed on Arun.

"Whatup, G. Come in," Jimmy said.

They silently made their way up to Jimmy's room, and he shut the door behind them.

"What's going on, man?" Jimmy asked as Gary sat down on the edge of his bed.

"I've just been cruising around and had a lot on my mind." Jimmy nodded. He allowed Gary some time to collect his thoughts. "First thing is, man, I gotta apologize for what happened tonight. I should have jumped in and stopped Sunny. But you know how he gets. Sometimes, you just can't talk sense into that guy."

"I know," Jimmy replied.

Gary looked at Jimmy curiously. "You're not upset?"

Jimmy paused. Strangely, animosity was not something he was feeling in the moment. "Nah. Maybe it was good that he got those shots in on me. I know he hates me for how I left him. But I did what I had to do. Maybe we can lay it to rest now."

"Yeah, I guess."

"I doubt that's all that you wanted to talk to me about," Jimmy said.

"Tonight, after the game, we went back to Sunny's place, and Sunny was pissed. And honestly, man, I don't think it had anything to do with you. I actually think he felt bad how the shit between the two of you went down. But anyways, him and Ajay started drinking. And then the blow came out. They've been doing that a lot lately."

Jimmy nodded. He wasn't surprised. "They were pretty fucked up," Gary continued. "And then Sunny finally told me what went down after his party that night, when his house got shot up. The guys that did it are big-timers in the game. They're suppliers, and they got into it with Sunny about not using them for his product. And you know Sunny. He ran his mouth, and they didn't like that, and they shot up his house to send a message."

"What did Sunny do?" Jimmy asked quietly.

"Sunny keeps a piece in the safe in his bedroom. And you remember how messed up Sunny and Ajay were. They must have been rolling on three or four different drugs that night. Sunny told me he wishes he hadn't done it." Gary paused as if he did not want to continue.

"What happened?"

"They found the guys," Gary finally replied. "And they shot back. They hit the boss' brother in the back. In the spine. He's paralyzed."

Jimmy's mouth suddenly felt dry, and he stared at Gary, knowing he was serious but hoping he wasn't. "So now what?"

"That's the thing, man," Gary replied. "Those guys haven't said nothing to Sunny. Not yet, at least. And I guess that's what's got Sunny so on edge. He don't know what the hell is going on."

Jimmy stood up from his desk chair and walked up to his window, looking out at the quiet evening. "You gotta get out." Gary didn't answer, so Jimmy turned around to face him. "You're not still thinking of working for him, are you?"

Gary stared down at his shoes and shook his head. "Nah, I'm not. It's just that…"

"It's just what? It can't be too hard of a decision, now that you know this."

It was Gary's turn to stand up, and he paced slowly back and forth.

"Sunny was your boy, wasn't he?" Gary said. "You guys obviously chilled for a while. I remember the things you used to tell me about how he would educate you on the game. And on life. And shit, man, he's done the same to me. He's tried to show me what he showed you. To live life on my own terms. And now, it's just hard to bail on him when he's at his lowest."

Jimmy understood that Gary's loyalty was unquestioned when he gave it. He walked slowly towards Gary, and when he reached him, he placed his hand on his shoulder until Gary finally met his gaze. "He was my boy. And he helped me learn things that I would have never been taught at school. But he also acts like he's more than who he actually is."

Gary stared at Jimmy. "What you mean?"

"Sunny's got family money. I don't know how much, or if his family still supports him or what. All I'm saying is that he can't relate as much to the struggle you've gone through. That we've gone through."

Gary continued to look at Jimmy without any words reaching his lips. "You know what's weird man?" Jimmy said, trying to put into words what he was feeling.

"When I was on the ground tonight after Sunny laid me out, I looked up at him, and I felt something. It wasn't hate or anything like that. I just felt bad for him. He's got demons, like we all do. But he still acts like he's the toughest guy on the block. I'm beginning to realize that all these guys who act so tough are usually the weakest of us all. Sunny might be scared of those guys that he fucked with, but there's something he's more scared of. He's scared of being found out to be a phony."

"Yeah, you might be right."

"I gotta ask you something," Jimmy said.

"Yeah, what's up?"

"I saw Sunny whispering something into Jessica's ear at the game today. Do you know what he said?"

Gary shook his head. "Sorry, bro, I don't know." He seemed disappointed that he couldn't answer the question.

Jimmy turned back towards his window, and towards the night that was as dark as it was quiet. "All good, bro. I think I already know."

29

WHEN JIMMY WOKE up the next morning, sore was an understatement. Jimmy's entire body hurt. He felt like he had just gone twelve rounds with Mike Tyson. He tried to stumble out of bed to get ready for school, but his body would not allow this, instead begging him for more rest to recover.

Jimmy was confined to his bed for the next few days. He got tired of scrolling through his phone, so he eventually turned it off and settled for a staring contest with the ceiling.

His mind was rambling from one thing to the next. From the biggest defeat that he had ever experienced on the basketball court, to the beat down that he'd taken at the hands of Sunny afterward. His thoughts drifted to Gary and how his loyalty was stopping him from cutting Sunny out of his life. The same loyalty that was usually reserved for him. He imagined what college might be like and wondered whether college coaches might still actually be interested in him, despite his reputation.

But his mind always seemed to want to return to one thing—one person. He still hadn't spoken with Jessica. He was scared of where the conversation would lead. There was only one outcome, if Sunny had told her.

As Jimmy continued to make best friends with his ceiling, eventually the thoughts became repetitive. Or rather, he became conscious that they were repetitive and that all this worrying wasn't doing anything to help the situation. On some level, he had always known this to be true. But as he lay in his bed, body aching in every muscle imaginable, mind weary from the constant anxiety these thoughts were causing—it just didn't make sense to him anymore.

Why am I thinking these thoughts?
Is me thinking about these things going to do anything to help the situation?
Is it even possible for me to stop if I wanted to?
And would I even want them to stop if I could?

It was as if this realization gave him an opportunity. The thoughts that had become so seductive had suddenly lost their allure.

If I thought about different things, would my life be different?
Is my reality simply conditioned by my thinking? Or is my thinking conditioned by my reality?
Is the tension that I feel in my body because of the burden that I carry in my head?

Heavy questions. But he was certain this was where *life* wanted to lead him. If he kept doing the same things, he would continue to get the same results.

On the deepest level, Jimmy knew that he could not answer these questions by rationalizations in his head. If he wanted richer and more truthful answers, he would have to go beyond the thinking mind.

He would have to live out this new truth. It was the only way. Day by day. Hour by hour. Moment by moment. Opportunities would be given. They always had been. They always would be. He just had to be open to the answers they would provide.

− 30 −

MIKE'S PARENTS WERE out of town that weekend, so it didn't take long for Mike to decide this would be a perfect time for an end-of-season wrap-up party. By the time Mike told Jimmy about it, he had already invited half their grade. "But if you can't come, we'll cancel it. We need the captain there," Mike had said to Jimmy on Friday.

Jimmy could only smile. He felt a lot better, and he didn't want to see the disappointed look on Mike's face if he said he couldn't make it.

When Jimmy's mom saw him in the kitchen on Saturday night, dressed as if he was going out, she gave him a stern look. "You should be resting."

Jimmy saw pure love and concern in her eyes, but still she was unwilling to forbid him from going out.

He walked up to her and gave her a big hug. "I'm okay, Ma. I promise. I'm only going to go for a bit."

He pulled into Panorama Ridge, heading towards the neighbourhood he had visited many times over the past year. He drove by Jessica's house on his way to Mike's, slowing down as he passed. Her bedroom light was still on.

Jimmy opened Mike's front door and stepped inside. There were more people than he had expected, and he had a sneaking suspicion that Mike had begun planning the party as soon as he found out that his parents were going to be out of town.

There was a staircase to Jimmy's right, leading upstairs to the bedrooms. At the far end of the house was the kitchen, where he could see stacked red cups and bottles of every type of liquor you could want. To his left was the living room, where the couches had been pushed up against the wall and a beer pong table had been set up. There was a crowd of people around the table, cheering.

"Jimmy!" someone yelled.

He turned and saw Mike stumbling up towards him. Unsurprisingly, Mike was already drunk. "Look who finally shows up." Jimmy laughed at Mike swaying in front of him. "Let's get a drink," Mike said, leading Jimmy to the kitchen.

Jimmy followed him to the table of booze and cups. Mike had also set up another table, which was full of chicken wings, a vegetable platter, and other finger foods. He took pride in hosting a party. Jimmy grabbed a red cup and looked at all the bottles of booze, then realized that he had no desire to drink. The booze just looked like poison in a bottle. After a moment's deliberation, he poured himself a cup of orange juice.

As he stood there, sipping his OJ, a few of his classmates approached and asked how he was feeling.

"Good, good. Hangin' in there."

Jimmy smiled when he saw Karnbir standing by himself by the kitchen sink. Jimmy approached and tapped him on the shoulder. Karnbir's smile almost took up his entire face. "Jimmy," he exclaimed. "How nice to see you!"

Jimmy laughed. "Nice to see you too, buddy. How are you doing?"

"I'm good. Amazing game. You were so good, how you could dribble the ball. I think the other team was mad that you were so good." And then Karnbir's face instantly turned into an expression of concern. "Are you okay though? I saw what happened in the parking lot. Who was that guy?"

"Just an old friend and some miscommunication. Nothing to worry about. How are you doing? It's nice to see you out. I told you one day we would party." He chuckled again.

Karnbir's smile reappeared as he held up a beer. "My first drink," he said proudly. "It doesn't taste very good, though. I don't know what all the fuss is about."

"Have a couple more, buddy. And then come see me," Jimmy said, grinning.

"Deal."

He headed out to the living room, where an intense beer pong game was underway. On the couches sat Mike, Karen, and Paul. Jimmy wasn't surprised that neither Jessica nor Gary was there.

"Jimmy, how's it going? How are you feeling?" Karen said, getting up to give Jimmy a hug.

"Like a million bucks," Jimmy replied. "Is Jess around?"

Karen shook her head. "I texted her, but she still hasn't replied. But she told me before that she would be here."

Jimmy nodded and turned his attention to Paul. "Whatup, G. Nice to see you out. To what do we owe the pleasure?"

"Just mourning that loss, man. We fought, though."

"Yessir, we did. Shit, and you're drinking," Jimmy said, noticing the bottle in Paul's hand.

"Already four deep, man. Just don't tell my parents." He laughed. "How you feeling tho, bro?"

"Yeah, I'm straight, man. Just got the wind knocked out of me."

"Should we have a little game of beer pong? Us two as partners? We gotta win something this year." He gave a wry smile.

"Let's do it."

Paul agreed to drink on Jimmy's behalf as they played Mike and Karen. Jimmy and Paul did end up finally getting their win.

And Paul celebrated like they had won the provincials. The booze definitely had loosened him up.

After an hour or so, Jimmy had accepted that Jessica probably wasn't going to show up. He scanned the party and observed how different everything seemed when he was sober in a room full of drunk people. It was nearing midnight, and the party was definitely in full force. He saw some of his friends dancing with girls they couldn't pluck up the courage to talk to when they were sober. The drink in their cup had a magical power. Jimmy wasn't certain whether it was for good or evil.

He reflected on all the drunken nights he'd had, but the memories were blurry and unfocused. He could remember more vividly all the mornings of waking up, after an alcohol-infused night, with regret and anxiety. He grinned to himself, understanding that only by going through the insanity could he become more sane.

He decided to call it a night and get home to his mom, who he knew was worrying about him, like she usually did. As he reached the front door, Paul approached.

"How do you do it?" Paul slurred.

Jimmy looked at him, confused by the question. He didn't reply immediately but instead surveyed Paul, who was swaying on the spot.

"You good, bro?" Jimmy asked him, smiling. "You look kinda drunk." He laughed to lighten the remark. "You need a ride home?"

"How do you do it?" Paul asked him again. Although he was drunk, his tone was serious.

"Do what?"

"You know. Do what you do."

"I don't know what you mean, man. But come on. Let me grab you some water, and then I'll drive you home. You just live around the corner, don't you?"

But Paul didn't move. He continued to stand, staring at Jimmy. They were near the front entrance and away from most of the other people. "How do you act like you do?"

"How *do* I act?"

"Like you have no fear. With anything. In basketball games, or with girls, or on the streets. If I had to spend a day hustling, I would fold like a bitch. But you don't. Sometimes, I wish I could be more like you."

Jimmy looked at him, stunned. "What do you mean? You're the class valedictorian, you're an athlete, you do all those extra-curricular activities. You're doing just fine. I think you're just a little drunk, man."

Paul shook his head. "Nah, I've felt this way for a long time. I just couldn't bring myself to say it because everyone thinks I have the perfect life. But it's not easy being me. People always expect me to be so fucking perfect, and I'm goddamn tired of it." His voice began to rise, and Jimmy could see some heads turning towards them. Jimmy didn't care, though. His eyes were fixed on Paul, knowing he was being sincere. "That's why Jess loves you, right? And not someone like me," Paul blurted out.

Jimmy glared. Even in his drunkenness, Paul seemed embarrassed by what he had just confessed. "I'm sorry, man," he mumbled. "I didn't mean it like that. It's just that you always seem so confident and sure of yourself." Paul's head drooped towards the floor as he spoke.

Jimmy took a deep breath. It wasn't just guys like Sunny who hid their insecurities. Their dysfunction manifested in different ways, but the breeding place was the same. He put his hand on Paul's shoulder, and Paul lifted his gaze.

"Listen, Paul, I ain't got it all figured out. Furthest thing from it. If you knew the shit that I've struggled with, you would think a lot differently. Maybe I got some qualities that you wish you had. But you got some qualities that I wish I had. We can wish all we want, but it's the wishing that's the problem. Maybe we gotta just accept what we got and make the best of it."

Paul nodded, but Jimmy could still see confusion and despair in his eyes. "Yeah, I know. Sometimes, I just get so frustrated, and I just want to run away from it all. But then I remember who I am, and all the things that people expect from me. The things I expect from myself. And so I shut all that shit out and get back to work to distract myself from it. But that shit stays with me. It's like a dark cloud hanging over my head."

Jimmy took a deep breath and looked around the room. The lights had been dimmed low, and the beer pong table had been shifted to the side to expand the dancing area. The music seemed to have gotten louder and the dancing more provocative. But Jimmy noticed the silence under the music, and a peace beyond the craziness. He focused his attention back on Paul, who was staring at him intently, hoping to get some answers that would cure him of his depression. He saw the pain and suffering in Paul's eyes like it was a reflection of his own.

"It can stop," Jimmy said, trying to explain the unexplainable. "I've been to the place where it has stopped. I'm just trying to find my way back."

Suddenly, Paul's eyes went wide as if something had drastically changed. Jimmy looked at him, concerned. "I'm gonna puke," Paul groaned. Without saying another word, he turned and ran towards the washroom.

Jimmy grinned. Maybe Paul would ask him again when he was sober. The more likely scenario was that they would never speak about it again.

He finished putting on his shoes, and headed outside to his

car. The evening was chilly but not unbearable. As he opened his car door, he contemplated how long it might be before the cops were called out for a noise complaint.

"Hey," a soft voice said from a few feet behind him. Jimmy recognized the voice instantly. He didn't turn around but remained facing his car, as he allowed the voice to echo, not in sound but in its vibration.

Finally, he turned around.

- 31 -

She was wearing grey sweats and a black hoodie. He took a step towards her but then stopped. Instead, he simply looked at her, no words reaching his lips. It was her who broke the silence.

"You leaving?" she asked.

Jimmy nodded. He heard his phone vibrate in his pocket and silenced it quickly. "Was going to. You don't seem dressed for a party."

Jessica grinned. "I guess not. I was going for a walk, and I ended up here. I wasn't sure if I wanted to come inside or not."

"Can I join you?" Jimmy asked. "On your walk?" She nodded.

They walked in silence away from the noise of the house. The further they walked, the more quiet the night became, until there was not a sound other than their breathing and footsteps.

Eventually, they reached an elementary school that they had visited a few times before. Jimmy slowed his pace as Jessica walked forward and towards a swing set.

She sat down on one and slowly began to allow the swing to sway back and forth. Jimmy leaned up against one of the poles and just watched her. He felt a breeze brush up against his face.

Again, it was Jessica who spoke first.

"How are you feeling?"

"I'm okay. No broken bones or anything. Just some bruises, but I'll be okay."

"I'm sorry I didn't come to see you earlier."

Jimmy nodded. "It's okay. I know you must have had your reasons."

Jessica stood up from the swing and walked towards Jimmy. He heard his phone buzz again in his pocket, and he clicked to silence it.

"Do you?" she asked so quietly that her words almost got lost in the wind.

Jimmy swallowed what saliva remained in his mouth. "Something that Sunny told you?"

Jessica looked away from Jimmy and towards the park in the background. She nodded. "I wanted to ask you about it, but I didn't want to hear you manipulate the truth."

Jimmy shook his head. "I won't. It's true. I was with a girl at Sunny's party." Jimmy looked at Jessica. Her expression didn't change. "I tried justifying it in my head. That we weren't together, or that telling you would only make things worse for everyone, and so what was the point. But the truth was that I was weak. The temptation got the best of me. It's been getting the best of me for a while now—not just with girls. I guess I've just been searching for something to make me feel complete. But when I'm with you, I feel complete. Even though those words probably mean nothing to you now."

Jessica took another few steps closer to Jimmy, until she was only a foot away. Jimmy wanted to hug her, but he resisted the urge, and the space between them remained.

"You make me feel complete too," she said. "But that's the problem."

"How can that be a problem?" Jimmy whispered.

"I want to feel complete without you. Everywhere I look, I see adults complaining about their lives and their relationships and their jobs. And I'm not saying that would happen with us. I just know that at one point, they thought they were in love too. I guess I just want to be content without needing anyone. Otherwise, I would be relying on someone else for my happiness. And I don't think I'm there yet."

Jimmy nodded. He felt his gaze drift down towards the gravel he was standing on. He could hear his heart thumping through his chest. He hoped Jessica could hear it too. "Yeah. I guess I get it," he said. "I just hate that this is how it would have to end between us."

Jessica took another step in, and now, she was only inches away from him. She reached forward and took his hands. Despite the chill of the evening, her touch was warm. "I remember my grandma told me something when my grandpa died," she said. "She told me that life isn't about possessing people. It's about experiencing them. And your presence has meant so much in my life."

Jimmy looked up, and Jessica was smiling. "You're going to do amazing things with or without me," she continued. "And we both know that. Something has shifted in you in the past little while, and we both know that you're ready."

"Ready for what?"

"You're ready for life. Not the life that your teachers want, or what Sunny wants, or what I want. But what you want. You're ready to be who you are. Who you've always been."

Jimmy stood there, understanding but not wanting to. He knew there weren't any more words to be spoken. He knew the silence would convey his pain. He managed a slight nod.

"Walk me home?" Jessica asked.

"Okay." His voice came out raspy, as if he hadn't said a word in days. This time, he did take her hand. And she let him. He heard his phone buzz a third time as they walked back, but he refused to let go.

His heart hurt, but not in a bad way. Maybe it was because he wasn't fighting the pain he was feeling. Or maybe it was because he knew he didn't have to suffer the pain alone. They shared it together.

When they finally reached Jessica's house, she turned to him and began to say something, but Jimmy stopped her. "Don't," he said quietly. "This walk was the perfect way to end it."

Her eyes twinkled in the moonlight as the delicate sounds of the evening night floated by. She looked at him with such a fierce love that Jimmy felt like he could die in that moment and be content. She held her arms out, inviting one last hug, and he accepted.

They finally let go, and then she turned and walked inside.

− 32 −

Jimmy returned to Mike's house, where his car was parked. The music had stopped, and it seemed like the party had wrapped up. He didn't know how long he had talked to Jessica. It had felt like time had ceased while they were together.

He sat in his car for a while, lost in neither thought nor impatience. He just sat there.

What finally startled him were the vibrations coming once again from his pocket. This time, he pulled out his phone and he saw it was a text message from Sunny: "CALL ME ASAP. IT'S GARY."

Jimmy looked at his other notifications, and he had three missed calls from Sunny and a missed call and voicemail from Gary. He felt his heart begin to beat rapidly, and there was a sudden sinking sensation in his stomach.

He called Gary first. After what seemed like an eternity, it went to voicemail. He hung up and then swiped on Sunny's missed call notification, and the phone began to ring.

"Jimmy!"

Sunny seemed out of breath and panicked.

"What's going on, man?" Jimmy asked.

There was a pause on the other line, and Jimmy could sense Sunny's hesitation.

"It's Gary," Sunny finally said. "Get down to the hospital. Surrey Memorial. ASAP."

Jimmy's vision began to go blurry, and everything around him spun. "What happened?" he struggled to say.

"Just get down here, now. I'll explain when you get here." Jimmy wanted to get his assurance that Gary was okay, but Sunny hung up before he had a chance to ask.

He began to put the keys into the ignition, but they slipped from his hand and fell between his seat and the middle console.

Everything around him refused to stop spinning. He took a deep breath, but it was to no avail. He felt nauseous, as if he was drunk, but he was sober, so he felt it completely.

Jimmy opened his car door, leaned outside, and vomited on the street in front of Mike's house. He could see the orange juice splattered on the pavement. He closed the car door and reached his hand down the side of the seat, searching for his keys. Luckily, they hadn't fallen completely underneath, and he managed to grab them.

This time, he was successful with the keys, and he opened his window to allow fresh air to circulate through his car. He took a deep breath, and then he took another. Things stopped spinning just enough for him to feel like he could drive. Surrey Memorial wasn't too far. He pulled out from the side of the road and headed in the direction of the hospital. All of his concentration went to the road, because every time his mind drifted to Gary, he felt the nausea and dizziness want to return.

He took the side streets to avoid any roadblocks or cop cars. In his condition, he had no business being on the road.

He finally had to turn onto King George Boulevard when he was only a few blocks away from the hospital. He had pulled up to the intersection, waiting to turn, when he saw it.

He was almost blinded by the flashing lights from the half dozen police cars that had blocked off an entire section of the road. At first, Jimmy suspected it was a roadblock, but he quickly realized that it wasn't. It was a crime scene.

Police officers were speaking to each other inside an area marked off by yellow police tape. Two were directing cars through. He saw the faces in the cars turn towards something that Jimmy couldn't yet see because a police car was obstructing his view. He saw jaws drop and eyes widen as cars slowly made their way past the scene. The police tried to usher the cars through as quickly as they could.

The light at the intersection turned green, but Jimmy couldn't turn onto King George Boulevard. He sat there, feeling paralyzed, fearing what he would see once he drove past. He heard a car honk from behind him.

Slowly, he turned and was now waiting to be ushered through. It was one-lane traffic, and cars were coming from the opposite direction.

Jimmy saw what appeared to be a husband and wife drive past the crime scene. As their car came towards his, he saw the wife turn to her husband with a horrified expression on her face. The husband simply shook his head and said something to her, then drove away.

The police officer waved at Jimmy's car to proceed. He obliged and slowly made his way past the police car that had been blocking his visual.

Jimmy saw a black-on-black Benz that he instantly recognized as Sunny's. It appeared to have done a 180 in the middle of the street and was now facing in the opposite direction. Bullet holes riddled the passenger side door, and the window had been blown out clean. Glass shards were scattered along the pavement.

He couldn't count how many bullet holes. A half dozen at the very least, probably more. The front tire had been shot flat, and the car sat sunken on its wheels. He could feel the urge to vomit again, and the car floor under him began to feel wobbly and unstable. Sweat broke out on his brow as his temperature rose.

Without a glance at the police offer, Jimmy drove through. Somehow, through his haze, he found himself parking outside the Surrey Memorial Hospital emergency entrance. His feet felt like they had taken control, since the rest of his body was failing him. He stepped out of his car and approached the entrance.

It was nearing 2:30 a.m., and as he walked into the lobby, there was a frantic energy. The seats were nearly full, and nurses rushed in and out of doors. Jimmy wanted nothing more than to turn around and leave, pretending all of this was a dream.

He spotted Gary's mom and little sister in the corner of the seating area, and his heart began to race once again. A hand was placed on his shoulder, and he turned around, only to see the bloodshot eyes of Sunny. His shoulders were slouched, and he looked defeated.

Jimmy didn't say anything and just stared into the lifeless eyes of the person he used to consider his mentor.

"Come outside with me," Sunny requested softly.

Jimmy didn't say anything or even nod, but he followed Sunny out the same way he had just entered. Sunny pulled a joint from his pocket and lit it once they stepped outside. He took a long, deep drag, then held it out. Jimmy shook his head. He couldn't.

"I'm sorry," Sunny said. Jimmy stood there, feeling helpless and numb. "For everything," Sunny continued.

Finally, Jimmy found his voice. "Is Gary okay?" He spoke so low that he could hardly hear the words himself.

"I don't know," Sunny replied. And then there was silence. Sunny continued to smoke the joint all the way to the tip, then threw the roach on the ground. "I gotta go," Sunny said.

"The police have some questions for me." Jimmy didn't respond. Sunny began to walk away but stopped after a few steps and turned back to him. "I wish it was me that they got."

Jimmy walked back into the hospital lobby, but this time, Gary's mom wasn't there. His sister had her back leaned up against the wall as she sat with her feet on the seat, hugging her knees close to her body. When she saw Jimmy, she quickly got to her feet and hugged him.

"Where's your mom?" Jimmy asked as he hugged her back.

She let go and looked up, her eyes brimming with tears. "The doctor called her in. He's going to be okay, right?"

The question hung in the air. He knew that he couldn't lie to her. "I don't know." And then he sat in the chair that had been occupied by Gary's mom, waiting for her to return.

Silently, he watched an older man approach the receptionist, and Jimmy could hear him complaining to her about how long he had been waiting. Jimmy couldn't hear what the receptionist said, but when the man returned to his seat, his face was contorted with rage. His eyes shifted around the waiting room suspiciously as he shook his head. Then the old man began muttering under his breath, as if having a conversation with himself. People sitting in his vicinity looked at him as if he was crazy.

Jimmy thought back to the last conversation he'd had with Gary, and how he should have done more and said more. Guilt washed over him as he remembered that he had introduced Gary to Sunny. He could feel the momentum of his mind driving him towards more thoughts, to punish himself.

But before it could, Jimmy sensed another voice in his head. It was quiet and almost inaudible. He took a deep breath, focusing on the exhale to calm his rapidly beating heart. It quieted just enough for him to hear the message.

Accept what you cannot change, and forgive when you cannot forget.

He took another deep breath. His attention returned to the old man, who was continuing to talk to himself, and Jimmy could hear most of the content was loathsome and negative. People continued to stare as if the old man was off his rocker and they were hoping he was here to get his medication. It dawned on Jimmy, though, that this old man was no crazier than the rest of them. Everybody in that waiting room was having a conversation with themselves. The only difference was that he was speaking aloud. And that wasn't much difference at all.

Without warning, Jimmy felt nauseous and faint once again. He clutched the sides of his chair to make sure he wouldn't fall off. The sounds from the hospital lobby seemed like they were turned all the way up to a ten, and he had never craved silence more than he did in that moment.

There were dim light fixtures hanging from the hospital ceiling, but in that instant, they became unbearably bright. He had to close his eyes, but in the darkness, he felt unsteady and weak.

His skin began to tingle all over, and then a burst of energy rushed through his body. All he could feel was the energy and nothing else. The darkness continued to surround him. He forgot where he was. He forgot who he was.

All that remained around him was a dark void and it was inviting him to come closer. He couldn't go closer, though, because suddenly, there was no him. It was just the experience of the experience, and his mind had gone completely quiet. It made no effort to interpret or analyze.

And then, finally, it all stopped. Everything. He didn't feel nauseous or weightless or off balance. He didn't feel anything because he had become everything. He had become quiet, like a slow, streaming lake after a violent storm.

Jimmy blinked his eyes open, and everything around him looked fresh and crisp, as if he were looking at life for the first time. It felt strange but familiar. New but sacred. It was as if he had gone on a long journey to an unknown land, and now, he had finally returned to what he knew was home.

Jimmy saw Gary's mom finally make her way back into the lobby. She was shaken and weak, like she could barely find the energy to walk. A doctor was comforting her, and Jimmy knew.

He knew that his friend, his brother, had passed on.

Without a thought, Jimmy stood up and walked over to Gary's mom, allowing the doctor to pass her on to him.

The doctor smiled warmly at Jimmy. "Are you family?" she asked. Jimmy nodded. She allowed Jimmy to lead Gary's mom away to sit down in the lobby.

Gary's mom was not crying, though. She seemed to be beyond tears. Her eyes were glazed over, like she had seen a ghost. Jimmy put his arm around her, and her head fell onto his shoulder. He put his other arm around Gary's sister, who had begun to sob again. He knew better than to say anything. No words, no matter how sincere, would be enough.

Instead, he closed his eyes and felt a sadness deeper than he had ever felt. But underneath the sadness, the peace and clarity remained. And as he held onto Gary's mom and sister, he felt a transcendent energy that could only have come from the *other side*. Jimmy just hoped they could feel it too.

After an amount of time that did not seem to matter, Jimmy led Gary's mom and sister to his car to drive them home.

As he pulled up in front of their house, Gary's mom turned to him. "Anytime he would speak about you, it almost sounded like he was bragging. For no reason other than that you chose him to be your best friend. He always told me that you were going to do amazing things. And I would just have to wait and see."

Jimmy just stared ahead, allowing the words to penetrate through him. With that, Gary's mom and sister walked out and home to their basement.

- 33 -

THE NEXT FEW days seemed almost like a blur. Jimmy's phone would not stop ringing, and text messages poured in from classmates and friends until he had to turn his phone off. He didn't want to hear condolences or have to offer them either. Words of sympathy seemed like a cheap substitute for what he was feeling.

He had told his mom what had happened when he woke on Sunday afternoon. Without a word, she pulled Jimmy in close and hugged him tighter than she had ever done before. He knew she was imagining it being her son. After that, she had gotten Jimmy's dad to drive her to visit Gary's mom.

Jimmy didn't go to school on Monday, nor did he attend on Tuesday.

Very few thoughts entered his mind during the days following Gary's death. It was almost as if when Gary had died, something inside of Jimmy had died as well. He couldn't explain it, nor did he have a desire to. The usual heaviness that lay on his shoulders had disappeared, along with the chronic tension that previously had found a home in the pit of his stomach. He felt empty, almost as if he didn't exist at all.

Wednesday morning came, and Jimmy was the first to wake in his house. It was still dark outside when he heard a thud at his front door. He opened the door and looked around to see where the noise had come from, then looked down and realized it was the morning newspaper being delivered. He retrieved the paper before walking back inside.

Pouring himself a bowl of cereal, he unrolled the newspaper and placed it on the kitchen table. Looking back at him from the front page was a picture of Gary.

A headline read:

GANG-RELATED SHOOTING LEAVES ONE DEAD AND THE COMMUNITY SEARCHING FOR ANSWERS

Jimmy flipped to the full-page story and began to read:

> Gary Dosanjh, high-school senior at Tamanawis Secondary, was shot dead on King George Boulevard near 94th Avenue early Sunday morning. The incident marks the 10th gang-related shooting in the first three months of the New Year and has left residents in Surrey neighbourhoods demanding more from the local government and police force.
>
> One resident who lives just a few blocks from where the shooting took place had this to say: "It's crazy. All this brown-on-brown violence. I blame the parents. They don't discipline their kids, and this is the outcome that we all have to deal with. I'm getting sick and tired of it. At least they hit the target this time. One of these days, an innocent bystander is going to get hit. I couldn't care less if they all kill each other off."
>
> The police have assured the public that this was a targeted shooting, and they are doing everything in their power to bring justice to the people responsible. We reached out to Surrey's mayor for comment and his office released this statement:

"We completely understand the public's frustration about the recent increase in gang-related shootings. As of today, I have authorized the hiring of 100 new police officers and the deployment of a separate task force that's primary focus will be to combat gang violence. We are committed to continuing the fight against drugs and gangs and everything that comes along with them."

Gary Dosanjh was the passenger in the vehicle at the time of the shooting. The driver was known to police. If you have any information regarding this shooting, please contact your local police station.

Jimmy stared at the article for quite a while. He didn't know what to think. He didn't want to think. He knew where his thoughts would lead him. And so he didn't. His mind remained blank as he closed the newspaper and rolled it back up. He put the elastic band back around it and placed the cylindrical package in the middle of the table, then finished the last few bites of his cereal and decided to go for a walk.

He had no set destination, deciding to let his feet take him wherever they wanted. He found himself walking down to the 7-Eleven that was only a few blocks from his house. When he got there, he dispensed a Slurpee, mixing six different flavours into the extra-large cup. He reminisced about Gary and him doing this as kids. He sipped the Slurpee as he continued walking.

He entered a cul-de-sac where they used to play ball hockey in elementary school, going until the evening darkness had made it impossible to see the ball. Jimmy stood in an adjacent driveway, reminiscing about one epic game they'd had. Kids from another school had challenged them to a match, and the intensity of the game made it feel like they were competing for the Stanley Cup. He remembered deking the goalie to score the winning goal and celebrating a little too exuberantly. The defenseman on the other team had taken offense and socked Jimmy right in the mouth. Jimmy had spat out a mouthful of blood and dropped his stick, and a brawl had ensued. It must have been a ten-versus-ten fight that day. No one took more victims than Gary. By the time the other team had scattered, both of Gary's fists were swollen like balloons from all the punches he had landed. Jimmy smiled, remembering how they had tried to think up what excuses they could tell their moms.

Finally, as he reached his street of 66th Avenue, and was heading home, he made a detour to his old elementary school. He stood on the uneven pavement of the outdoor basketball court, which had crooked white lines and an even more crooked basketball hoop. He remembered the day he and Gary had become best friends. It was in grade two, on a day not unlike this one.

Jimmy was shooting three-point shots when Gary approached him.

"Hey."

"Hey," Jimmy responded without paying him any attention.

Gary stood there, watching Jimmy play for a while, before the ball clanged off the rim and ended up at Gary's feet.

"Go on. Let's see what you got," Jimmy told him. "You're a big boy, but do you got the touch?"

Gary heaved up a three-point shot that clanged off the backboard. Jimmy chuckled as he collected the ball.

"Maybe shooting isn't your strong point. But I'm sure you can get your fair share of rebounds," Jimmy said.

"Yeah, nobody is going to take the ball away from me," Gary said proudly.

"Alright then, let's see what you got."

Jimmy arrived home with a quiet mind and a peaceful heart. He went to his room and sat on his desk chair, gazing out the window, until the sunlight began to fade. Without warning, a burst of sadness overcame him. He did not resist it, and he felt himself falling into the feeling.

He found tears swimming in his eyes as his vision became blurred and hazy. He did not wipe them, instead allowing them to flow down his cheeks and down to his lips. They were salty and warm, and they tasted like sadness should.

He heard a knock on his bedroom door. "Come in," Jimmy said. The remnants of the tears still clung to his cheeks.

The door creaked open slightly, and Coach Dhillon's head poked through. Principal Nelson, Ms. Chohan, and Mr. Pratt followed him in.

"Jimmy," Coach Dhillon said quietly. "How are you doing?"

A smile crept onto Jimmy's lips. That was the question to ask, wasn't it? *How are you doing?* After all, what else could someone ask in a situation like this? "I'm okay," he replied.

Things became silent as they all stared out Jimmy's window, no words seeming quite appropriate for the moment.

After a few minutes, Principal Nelson broke the silence. "Jimmy, this is a difficult time for all of us. And we will support you and your classmates in any way that we can. We understand if you need to take some time off school to mourn your friend and do it the way you feel is best."

"Thank you." He continued to look out the window but instinctively knew they wanted to get more out of him.

"Do you know when you plan to come back to school?" Ms. Chohan asked kindly.

"I can communicate with some of your teachers to make sure

that you don't fall too far behind. You've done such a tremendous job of catching up."

This time, Jimmy did turn his chair around to look at Ms. Chohan. She had mother-like instincts, and Jimmy knew she was worried about him. He smiled warmly, hoping that his smile would convey to her that he was okay.

"That would be great. Next week, I'll be back." She returned his smile and nodded.

Mr. Pratt had yet to say anything. He stood at the very back of the room and simply stared at Jimmy with a curious expression.

Jimmy's guests seemed to accept that there wasn't much else they were going to get out of him. Principal Nelson walked over and put his hand on Jimmy's shoulder. "Feel better, Jimmy," he said. "We will see you soon."

He nodded. "Thank you, sir."

When they turned to leave, he realized there was someone he did want to talk to. "Mr. Pratt, can I talk to you?"

Mr. Pratt turned to his colleagues. "You guys go ahead. I'll find my own way back."

They nodded and left, and Mr. Pratt took a seat on the edge of the bed. Jimmy didn't immediately say anything. He didn't even know what he wanted to say to Mr. Pratt. He just knew that the counsellor's presence always seemed to comfort him.

He had known that Coach Dhillon, Ms. Chohan, and Principal Nelson were searching for something to say when they were there. But Mr. Pratt wasn't. He was sitting there, basking in the silence. Jimmy appreciated that he wasn't trying to force anything.

"I never got a chance to thank you," Jimmy said. "For stepping in after the basketball game and holding Sunny back from kicking me that night."

Mr. Pratt chuckled. "I was surprised at my own strength. I guess I haven't lost all of it quite yet."

"He was with Gary the night he got shot," Jimmy said. "Sunny, I mean. It was because of him that Gary got shot. Problems he had with some *gangsters.*" Mr. Pratt offered a slight nod of his head but said nothing, so Jimmy continued. "It's been strange these past couple of days. I'm sad, but I'm not depressed. A small part of me feels like I should be. I mean, I just lost my best friend. I should be broken and miserable and hurting, shouldn't I?"

Mr. Pratt smiled slightly. "Sometimes, the greatest losses become an opportunity for our greatest openings. Emotions come as they will, but there is a deeper place beyond that, and I believe you are beginning to find it. That place cannot be touched by emotions, or anything else. Most people allow themselves to become consumed with surface-level emotions because the feeling is seductive. It's an attempt to feel something that for them feels truly real. But emotions are fleeting, like waves on the surface. The truly real *Is*. It just *Is*."

Jimmy pondered Mr. Pratt's answer for a few moments. "I haven't been thinking as much. And even when I do, the thoughts don't feel heavy, like they used to. It feels almost like I'm in a trance. But even that doesn't seem like the right word. It feels like…" He paused, contemplating what it was that he felt. "It feels like I'm alive. For the first time." Mr. Pratt's eyes danced with jubilation, but his smile was soft and gentle.

They both became quiet as they listened to the sounds drifting through Jimmy's open window. They could hear the whistling of cars drive by, and kids laughing as they played in the park across from Jimmy's house. They both paid attention to the silence from which the sounds were born. There was a pleasant sensation of tranquility that flowed through Jimmy's bedroom.

Mr. Pratt stood up. "I should be heading out, Jimmy, but there is something that I wanted to speak with you about, and now seems like as good of a time as any."

"Yes sir, what is it?"

"As you know, I used to play on the Canadian national basketball team. And I made quite a few connections during this time. And one of my best friends is the head coach of the University of Victoria. He has heard, of his own accord, about your talent, and I confirmed to him that there is no doubt in my mind you would excel playing at the next level. He's told me that if you can keep your grades up by the end of the year, he wouldn't hesitate in offering you a scholarship to play basketball there."

Jimmy knew that Mr. Pratt had done more than what he was letting on to assure him a spot. He must have vouched for him personally. But he also knew that this was what he wanted. There was no denying it anymore.

"Thank you, sir."

-34-

GARY'S FUNERAL WAS arranged for Sunday morning, and his mom decided that she wanted it to be intimate, with only close friends and family. However, she allowed Principal Nelson to arrange a memorial that would be held in the high school gymnasium on Saturday morning, where everybody was welcome to attend and pay their respects.

Jimmy decided to walk to the school on that quiet Saturday morning, like he used to do before he drove everywhere. It was the beginning of March, and the first flowers had begun to bloom in anticipation of Spring. Jimmy could taste the sweet fragrance in the air as the sun shone down on him. The sky was a piercing blue, and it was clear. Seagulls soared above him.

When Tamanawis finally became visible, he saw people scattered throughout the parking lot. More people than he had expected. He felt his pace slow as he indulged in the last few moments of solitude.

His classmates made their way over to Jimmy when they saw him, and hugs and words of encouragement were shared. He could feel the vibrations of sadness echo throughout the lot, and many tears were shed.

In the midst of the crowd, he saw Karnbir standing by himself. Jimmy approached, and when Karnbir saw him, his face lit up. His smile reminded Jimmy of Gary's. So genuine and sincere, a smile that filled his face.

"Hi, Jimmy."

"Hey, Karnbir."

He could tell Karnbir was searching for something to say in a time and place where no words were needed. Jimmy placed a hand on his shoulder and stared into his eyes. "No need to say anything. You being here is enough." And then they shared an embrace before Jimmy continued to make his way through the crowd.

He found Gary's mom speaking with Principal Nelson. When they saw him, the principal waved him over. "Jimmy," he said. "I've been trying to call you, but your phone continues to go to voicemail."

Jimmy nodded but didn't offer any explanation. Before Principal Nelson could continue, Gary's mom ushered Jimmy off to the side so they were alone. "Jimmy," she said quietly. "There isn't anyone here who knows my boy like you do. Will you share a few words today when we gather together in the gymnasium?"

Jimmy stared at her blankly. "Uhh. I mean, I don't have anything prepared or anything."

"Please." Her voice was soft but pleading, her eyes red from tears and lack of sleep.

He smiled and nodded. "Of course."

She hugged him. "Thank you."

The crowd began to file into the gymnasium, but Jimmy hung back. He could see his classmates, teachers, and other people he recognized from the neighbourhood enter as he observed from a distance. He saw Mike and Karen, followed by Jessica and Paul.

The bleachers were completely full, and the rows of chairs that led onto the basketball court were completely occupied. People were also up against the walls, standing wherever they could find room.

There was a small space for a projection screen that was set up with a platform and a microphone. A half dozen chairs next to the platform faced the crowd of people. They were occupied by Principal Nelson, Coach Dhillon, Gary's mom, Gary's sister, and an elderly woman Jimmy assumed was Gary's grandmother. There was one empty seat, and when Gary's mom spotted him, she called out, "Jimmy, this seat is for you."

Jimmy nodded and made his way over. Once he sat down, he looked out into the crowd and saw Mr. Pratt sitting in the front row, hands neatly folded in his lap.

As he continued to scan the gymnasium, Jimmy saw Ajay and Sunny, who were hardly visible, sitting in the top corner of the bleachers. He locked eyes with Sunny and felt a surge of energy course through his body. He allowed the energy to rush through him until he regained his natural state. With his skin still tingling, he gave the smallest of nods in their direction, and they both nodded back.

Principal Nelson stood up and approached the platform. "Thank you all for joining us to celebrate the life of a fine young gentleman who was taken from us far too soon: Gary Dosanjh." He paused and shuffled some papers sitting on the platform.

"As evident from today's turnout, Gary was well loved and well respected in the community. His classmates would describe him as a gentle giant who had a smile as big as his heart. Gary also excelled on the basketball court and was a key component to the successful basketball season Tamanawis had this year. It wouldn't have been a surprise to anyone if Gary had continued on to play in post-secondary." He continued to shower praise upon Gary for the next five minutes. Some of it was true, but most of it was exaggerated, and most people in the gym knew this.

"And now before we continue on with other speeches, please direct your attention to the projection screen for a slideshow."

The lights of the gymnasium were dimmed low, and the projection screen was switched on.

The slideshow began with pictures of Gary as a baby. To no one's surprise, he'd been a gigantic infant, with the same distinguishable flat nose and wide mouth. As Gary got older, his love and affection for his mom became evident. There were a few photos of him as a boy, showing him clinging to his mom's leg. Jimmy knew this was probably around the time that Gary's dad had abandoned their family.

And then, flashing onto the projection screen, was their grade seven school picture. It was the same photo that Jessica had retrieved months back to show Jimmy. He stared up at the twelve-year-old versions of him and Gary, and a smile touched his lips. They had their arms around each other's shoulders, and the sincerity of their smiles beamed from the photo.

The pictures graduated to Gary becoming bigger and bigger, until he towered over anyone else in a photo. Nearly half the images from high school onwards included Jimmy. He gazed up at the screen, feeling incredibly blessed by all the experiences he had shared with Gary. The final photo, which remained illuminated on the screen longer than any other, was from their last basketball Christmas dinner at Mike's house.

It was not unlike their grade seven school photo, as they each had an arm wrapped around the other's shoulder, and smiles that seemed to reach from ear to ear. Gary was holding a red cup in one hand that definitely didn't contain water. Jimmy was tilting his head upwards, and he remembered joking to Gary that they were basically the same height. On Jimmy's left stood Jessica. She was gazing lustfully up at him, and he realized these were the two people he had cared for more than anyone else in his life. He turned his attention away from the screen and towards where he knew Jessica was sitting. She was looking directly back at him.

Once the slideshow concluded, Principal Nelson once again rose and approached the platform. He introduced Coach Dhillon, who spoke some kind but predictable words. As he walked back to his chair, Jimmy observed tears streaming down his coach's face.

"And now, we will hear from Gary's best friend and basketball teammate, Jimmy," Principal Nelson said.

Jimmy felt every eye in the entire gymnasium shift towards him. He witnessed himself standing up, and he slowly but deliberately walked to the microphone as Principal Nelson sat back down.

Standing on the platform, he gazed out at all the eyes that were focused solely on him. He looked around at all the serious and subdued faces. Some of them in the gymnasium knew Gary quite well, but there were many others who hardly knew him at all. Jimmy knew that Gary hadn't associated with very many people. So what was the deal with the big crowd? Maybe some of them came simply because they had nothing better to do today. Maybe Gary was a friend of a friend. Maybe some thought that they cared. Hell, maybe some of them actually did care.

And so he stood there on that Saturday afternoon, as classmates, friends, and strangers looked on. Then he cleared his throat and leaned into the microphone. "I've known Gary ever since I can really remember. And uh... He was a great guy and a great friend. He was always smiling. And uh... I feel very fortunate to have known him for the time that I did. What happened was a tragedy."

And then Jimmy paused and took a step back from the microphone. He closed his eyes for just a moment, took a slow and steady breath, and regained his centre.

He forgot about the crowd of people. This speech was not for their benefit. He didn't care about being nice or polite or delivering words that were appropriate. All he cared about was the truth. He stepped back in towards the microphone. When he spoke, his voice was deliberate, and the words came without thought.

"Gary was loyal. Loyal to a fault. And in the end, maybe it was his loyalty that cost him his life. If he cared for you, he would ride with you. No matter the stakes. It is death that brought us here today. Death is the great equalizer, isn't it? It doesn't pay any mind to who we are or what we are. It will come for us, whether we are ready for it or not. Some of us are terrified of the thought, and you can observe it in the way that they live. The fear of death trickles through every pore of their life. They're in a rush because they know their time is limited. But then there are others…"

Jimmy found Mr. Pratt in the crowd and observed the peaceful aura that emanated around his being. He looked serene, peaceful, present.

"The others. Those who are the exception rather than the rule. Those who have learned to accept the unacceptable. Those who do not shy away from what must be confronted. Those who do not dwell on what cannot be changed." He paused.

"I'm going to miss Gary like crazy. All the stupid shit that we've done. All the joints we've smoked, and the burgers we've munched. I read the newspaper article that came out a few days after Gary's death. It talked about the war against drugs and the war against gangs and how the people at the top are going to use Gary's death as yet another example to fight this *'senseless violence.'* It talked about how we need more police, more programs, more attention.

"These fuckin' chumps don't recognize what's really going on. And they can't recognize what's going on because they're lost themselves. We want to wage a war out there because we have a war happening right here." Jimmy pointed at his heart.

"We love the conflict, like we love the drama. It's addicting, and it captures our attention, and we focus our energy in the wrong place. We can't shy away from what's really going on anymore. We have to feel the pain until it becomes unbearable, and then, even then, we can't look away. We got to feel it. We got to feel it all the way through. Only then can we acknowledge the reality of the situation, and see things for what they really are.

"So if you really want to honour Gary's legacy, let's do it by living truer to ourselves. Because we can cry, and mourn Gary's death, but tomorrow is still going to come, and when we wake up, we'll have a choice to make. Would you rather be at war with yourself and at peace with the world, or at peace with yourself and at war with the world?"

And with that, Jimmy walked back to his chair.

- 35 -

HE DIDN'T HANG around the parking lot, where most of the people remained, sharing their memories of Gary. Instead, he walked up the gravel hill, past the fields and in the direction of the cage. He didn't have a basketball, but it was where his feet decided they wanted to go.

The chatter from the parking lot slowly dissipated as he walked further and further, until he couldn't hear it at all. When he reached the top field, he could finally see the cage in the distance. He took a slow, deep inhale, as if he were breathing it in. He wasn't in any hurry to reach the cage. Each step he took that led him in that direction was slow and unhurried. His eyes were fixated on the cage, his destination, but he knew rushing there would only diminish the walk. He continued to feel the peace in his heart like it was the most important thing in the world. Because he knew that it was. Maybe that's how it was with for any goal he was trying to reach. Impatience and sheer determination may get him there faster, the same way he could sprint to the cage. But he knew life wasn't a sprint. It was a marathon. And all that was important was to continue to put one foot ahead of the other in the direction he was intending to go. And wherever he ended up, and whatever he ended up doing, the most important thing was how he got there.

He did finally reach the cage. Slowly, he lifted up the latch to unlock the door, remembering all the times Gary had struggled with it. The breeze rustled the leaves of the trees, and it sounded as if they were laughing at the seriousness of the day.

When Jimmy entered, he turned back in the direction of the school. He had never realized how the cage was elevated above the school, like the peak of a mountain. He contemplated his school like it was the countryside, observing the green and landscaped grass of the soccer and baseball fields, where he used to run around as a kid. In the distance, he could see his elementary school and even the road that led up to his house.

He looked down at his schools and the fields and the roads that, if nothing else, were the remnants of his teenage years. His body became light, his gaze soft, and he craned his neck upwards, feeling the expansiveness of everything around him.

He saw a silhouette in the distance, exactly like he had seen so many times in the past. It had to be Gary coming to join him for a workout. Jimmy's heart began to race, and he listened to each heartbeat as if it was his favourite song that he was hearing for the final time.

The silhouette continued to walk in the direction of the cage. Quickly, Jimmy realized it was too small to be Gary, but his heart continued to race. He closed his eyes and felt his mind empty of any expectations. He indulged in the darkness, forgetting where and who he was. His heart returned to its rhythmic pattern, and he felt a coursing of energy. The energy didn't feel solid but rather like it was dancing with joy. His feet weren't touching the ground; instead, they melted into it, as if it were also a part of him.

He slowly opened his eyes. The grass was greener, the sky was bluer; the world was simpler. His eyes returned to the silhouette, but now she could be recognized. Jessica had reached the cage door and was unlatching the lock.

She walked in but didn't immediately say anything. Jimmy just stared at her as she approached slowly. And then, before a word was spoken, she was standing directly in front of him. She didn't look sad, or upset, or concerned. Her expression was blank, but it was intense. Without being aware of it, Jimmy wore the same expression.

And then she hugged him. And he hugged her back. She leaned her head against his chest, and he knew she was crying. He couldn't hear her crying, but he could feel her sadness, as if the physical contact connected them on a deeper level. Jimmy closed his own eyes and lowered his head onto the top of her shoulder. Her hair brushed against his face, and he felt his own tears now. She hugged him tighter, and he did the same.

Finally, they separated.

"I can't believe he's gone," Jessica whispered. Jimmy looked away from her and nodded. "I've been trying to call you," she said.

"Yeah, sorry. I just needed some time, I guess. I had my phone turned off. I just couldn't really talk to anyone."

She went silent as Jimmy walked over to the basketball hoop. He put his hand on the pole and felt the cold steel against his fingertips.

Jessica walked over to join him, saying, "We've had a lot of good memories, haven't we?"

"Yeah, we have. Memories we will never forget." He wasn't certain what else to say. Jessica wasn't his girlfriend anymore, and even though he still appreciated her presence, something was different. He could tell as she was standing there looking up at him that she wanted him to open up and talk to her. And he knew he could tell her about Mr. Pratt's offer to help with his post-secondary plans, or how he'd felt when he learned Gary had passed on, or how he'd felt this indescribable peace over the past week. But the urge to confide in her had abandoned him. It might have been because she had broken up with him, but he sensed a different reason. His relationship with her was a lot like Gary's now—just a memory.

"I should get going," he finally said.

She seemed disappointed but felt there was something different about Jimmy. He seemed more detached, almost like a part of him was missing. "Are you okay?" Jessica asked.

He smiled. His eyes shifted to the surrounding trees, around to the parking lot, and then up to the sky. "Yeah. I'm okay."

Jimmy arrived home to his mom cooking dinner and his dad sitting on the couch, a drink in hand. He walked over to his mom and gave her a kiss on the cheek. "Thanks for everything, Ma." She smiled, her heart full and content.

He grabbed an empty glass, then walked over to the couch to join his dad. He poured himself a thick shot of Crown Royal. "Tell me about when you played cricket, Pops."

His dad grinned. In that moment, Jimmy felt love in his home that he had never felt before. It was the same house and the same people but a different vibration. It was held in his heart.

He spent the next hour listening to his dad tell him about different matches he had played as a young man. He even brought out an old photo album and showed pictures from those days. Jimmy couldn't believe how much he resembled his teenage dad.

And then suddenly, Jimmy remembered something. He excused himself and walked slowly up to his room, his mind as quiet as his heart.

He opened the door to his bedroom and pulled out his backpack from underneath the bed. Unzipping it, he pulled out his phone and turned it on. Instantly, he was alerted to all of his missed notifications, which he ignored. He clicked on the voicemail button, and a dozen or so different voicemails popped up, but he scrolled all the way down and found the one he was searching for. It was from Gary, only an hour before he had died.

Jimmy pressed the play button and put the phone to his ear. Gary's voice spoke: "Jimmy, whatup, G. I've had a few drinks at home now, and I'm feeling good." There was a pause, and he knew Gary had been collecting himself before continuing.

"I just wanted to let you know that I'm about to meet up with Sunny right now, and I'm gonna tell him what's up. I'm gonna tell him that I already got someone in my life who is showing me the way. Because that's what you've been doing your entire life for me since my pops left. And I know you're still figuring out your own shit, but there ain't no one who I want in my corner more than you. You see things that other people don't. I just hope you can go easier on yourself, and realize that you're something special. Not because you're any different than any of us, but because you've figured out what's real, and now you're just learning how to deal with it. But yeah, anyways, man, I'm gonna try to stop by Mike's place after I talk with Sunny. Hopefully I'll see you there, bro. Love you, man."

Jimmy stared down at his phone. And then he began to laugh. Not for any other reason except that he saw the humour in life in that moment. It all seemed so simple, like the answer had been right in front of his eyes this entire time. The reality of that particular moment was what life was. And the quality of that moment would determine the quality of his life. Because what else was life but a collection of moments, in a forever-happening and eternal process.

He gently placed his phone on his bedroom desk, then gazed out his bedroom window, noticing everything but nothing at the same time. He sat down on his chair and picked up *The Alchemist*, turning to the page where he had last left off. The words on the page were a pointer to something that could never be described in words. But Jimmy wasn't looking for any more knowledge or wisdom. He had exhausted that avenue and knew it was a dead-end in every single direction. He wanted to read, simply because he enjoyed the story.

THE END

Surrey Jack

That quiet boy you ignored as a kid
Had anger building up inside of him

Finding solace in role models who are "self-made"
And "self-paid"

They were never gangsters
It was just the only place they found their own kind

Picking fights to hide their insecurities
Buying up the bar to get that one girls attention

Money is their motive
A lack of choice keeps them on the street

How can we blame them
When it's us that made them

If you want to clean up the streets
Understand we are the streets

So before pointing the finger
Close your eyes and breathe
And know we must be the change that we want to see

Look into the pit of your being
And notice your own anger
Your own aggression
Your own insecurities

Theirs is simply a magnification
Of what already exists

So before you mock
Observe

Before you belittle
Empathize

And before you fear
Love

Then maybe
Just maybe

We'll embrace them as the sons and brothers
Like they've only ever been

~Michael Bains

Afterword

Thank you for reading *Hooped*, a book that means a lot to me for a number of reasons.

As a child who loved to write, I dreamed of becoming an author. Over the years, I started and stopped writing a handful of books. None felt quite right, and I knew I'd only ever be able to release a book that truly came from my heart.

I often find that my days are better when I write. Writing allows me to express myself without a filter or a fear of being judged. I've always known that I have a deep heart and something to say. My outlet for these is writing.

I believe all of us should be artists in one way or another. Creativity has become underappreciated, and competition an obsession. We are constantly urged to do things with an end goal in mind, and very often, we forget to simply appreciate the journey.

Words are powerful, so whether the words come from a book, a song, or spoken conversation, their influence is limitless. I have had no formal education related to writing since my Grade 12 English class. But what I do have is access to a genuine place within myself where the words come from. My hope is that this book was able to connect with you on that same level.

I have created a separate page on Facebook and Instagram with the handle @HoopedTalks. My intention with this page is to showcase how words inspire our community. I will be releasing a weekly episode of the "Pursue Your Passion Series," where individuals will write in their own words, the importance of pursuing a passion.

If you would like to submit your own story for the "Pursue Your Passion Series," you can email hooped@michaelbains.ca. This page will be a compilation of words that come directly from us.

Also, word of mouth is definitely the best form of marketing; so if the novel resonated with you, please consider telling a friend or two. Also, if you wish to share the book on your social media, please tag @HoopedTalks and use the hashtag #HoopedTalks. You can visit the website www.michaelbains.ca to learn more about the projects I will be working on in the future.

What I've realized through this process is that all I can be is a person who delivers a message that I could never take personal credit for. The greatest service I can be to the world and myself is one who follows my passion with sincerity. I hope this book inspires you to do the same.

Yours truly,
Michael Bains

About The Author

Michael was born and raised in Surrey, BC, Canada, where he lived until his early twenties. He has since moved away from his hometown, but those early years continue to be a defining period in his life.

Currently 29, he lives in the Yaletown district of Vancouver, where you can usually find him at the local library, or walking the seawall. He enjoys staying physically active and is an avid reader and writer. *Hooped* is his first published novel.

Michael's website can be found at www.michaelbains.ca. Drop by the site to offer feedback on any of his writing, to learn how you can help support the book, or to leave him a note about something else. You can also email Michael at hooped@michaelbains.ca.

Manufactured by Amazon.ca
Bolton, ON